*She was the same vis[ion]
dreams.*

Ben ran his fingers through his hair, feeling as if he were in a dream. It had to be her. His senses throbbed as he stood near enough to smell the lilac fragrance she wore. She was even more beautiful up close. . .

"Can I help you?" her tone was cool, interrupting his thoughts.

"Yes, I. . .ah. . ." Ben felt idiotic, but he had to know for sure. "My name is Ben Thackeray and I. . .could you take your hat off again?"

"What?"

"Please?" He tried to put his earnestness and uncertainty into his face, hoping she wouldn't deny his request. Reluctantly, she swept off her hat, cocking a questioning eyebrow at him.

There it was.

Ben sucked in his breath when he saw what he had suspected. The oddly shaped birthmark on her right temple seemed to jump out at him.

Her hand flew up of its own accord to cover the mark. She stared at him, her eyes wide. He came back to his senses then, realizing that he had frightened her. *You're such a cad,* he berated himself silently. *Couldn't you have been a little more subtle?*

"I'm sorry to appear so rude." He started to run his fingers through his sun-bleached hair, then stopped himself. He hadn't felt this nervous the first time he piloted the ship. The way she was staring at him didn't help matters any, either. He didn't like the wariness that lurked in her sage green eyes, as if he might actually harm her. She reminded him of a fawn he had startled out of its hiding spot once as he hiked through the woods.

"I'm sorry I frightened you," he apologized again. "I just had to be sure it was you. You are Raine Thomas. . .?"

AMY ROGNLIE is thrilled to have her first novel published. This wife and mother drew on her home in Colorado for scenes in her story that assures readers God is love and He is ever willing to forgive.

Along Unfamiliar Paths

Amy Rognlie

Heartsong Presents

*Dedicated to the memory
of my beloved sister,
Sarah P. Weston
who ran with patience
the race set before her and
victoriously traveled the ultimate
Unfamiliar Path.*

We'll see you again soon, Sarah!

A note from the author:
*I love to hear from my readers! You may correspond with me
by writing:* **Amy Rognlie
Author Relations
PO Box 719
Uhrichsville, OH 44683**

ISBN 1-57748-321-9

ALONG UNFAMILIAR PATHS

Cover illustration by Chris Cocozza.

PRINTED IN THE U.S.A.

prologue

On the Atlantic Ocean
February 1903

The clanging bells jerked him from a deep sleep seconds before the pounding on his cabin door began. Leaping from his bunk, the dark-haired sailor wrenched the door open, finding nothing but his captain's voice echoing down the hall. "She's going down! The ship is going down! This is not a drill."

The man snatched up his life jacket, pausing for one precious moment to assure himself that the locket was still there, lying warm against his chest. He felt a dark feeling of premonition, a sense that mortal danger hovered over him. Flying up to the top deck, he ripped the object from the chain that had held it close to his heart for so long. Pressing it into his captain's hand, he felt a weight lift off his shoulders.

For a moment, though, tears sprang to his eyes unbidden. *Surely now she would understand. . .* A surge of water over the deck interrupted his thoughts. Pulling himself together, he turned to the task of evacuating the ship.

He reassured each fearful passenger with a smile, ignoring the acrid smoke that stung his nostrils and the memories that wounded his heart. Lowering the last woman to the safety of the lifeboat, he caught a quick movement out of the corner of his eye. He whirled, but it was in vain. The hands of his nemesis were too swift. Staggering from the hard slash across his face, the burly sailor felt himself being shoved over the railing.

He snatched at the hands that were thrusting him downward, clinging desperately to them. "It won't matter," he gasped. "The papers are—" His hands slipped and he plunged silently toward the icy water, blinded by his own blood. The balsa wood in his life preserver struck him under the chin as he hit the water, throwing his head back with such force he was knocked unconscious.

The frigid cold of the water brought the sailor back to consciousness at last. . .and filled him with terror. How long could he last in this icy grave?

How foolish he had been, to think he could win by his own rules. He groaned aloud as his father's angry face rose up to taunt him. And the locket. Surely it wouldn't be too late. . . *God, I can't die this way!*

His tears spilled over, bathing his frozen cheeks in momentary warmth. Did anyone even know or care that he was dying out here? He shivered violently, colder than he ever thought possible. And the thick, unnerving quiet. No sound, except his own labored breathing. Was this what it felt like to die? He would just slip quietly under the water, and no one would ever know. . .

God will know. A new wave of dread washed over him at the thought. He wasn't ready to face God.

Desperation lending strength to his numbed senses, he raised his head an inch to peer across the inky waters and into the frozen night sky, only to have his last hope fade away. The lights of the ship were gone. Gone! Like a young man's dreams of the future. Fear rose in his throat, ready to strangle him.

"God!" He cried out to the One he had so long forgotten. "Save me!"

one

London, England
1906

•

Ben Thackeray leaned back in his chair with a weary sigh. Lifting his eyes to the window overlooking the wharf, he absently scanned the activity as his mind continued to mull over the problem at hand. *It just may be that I'll have to go to New York myself,* he mused. *There are just so many loose ends, so many things that could go wrong, so many buttons. . .*

Buttons? He found himself staring distractedly at the back of a woman's dress. *There must be a hundred buttons down the back of that dress,* he thought as she moved past his window. He watched a moment longer as she picked her way across the pier.

Catching a glimpse of her face, he felt his mouth go dry. He turned back to his desk, running a shaking hand through his hair. "Get back to work, old chap," he muttered out loud to himself. "It couldn't be her after all this time."

Images of a slender waist and soft lips teased his mind as he studiously bent over his papers. Giving up after a few minutes, he unfolded his long legs from under the desk. From his viewpoint, he could see halfway down the waterfront. Ah, there she was.

He watched her as she spoke to an elderly fisherman, enjoying the graceful gestures of her hands. He saw her turn to leave, her shoulders slumping. His heart leapt as she turned toward him.

You're imagining things, he told himself sternly. *It just can't be. . .*

Now staring in earnest, he tried to decide what it was about the woman that compelled him. Was it the glimpse of chestnut-colored curls. . .the curve of the jaw. . .the smooth forehead just visible under her hat. . .that was it!

He had to see her without the hat, he decided.

&

Raine Thomas glanced at the leaden sky. *It's now or never,* she told herself firmly.

Lifting her heavy skirts an inch as she edged around the mud puddle that stood between her and the wharf, she grimaced at the muck. It reminded her of the barnyard back home.

It wasn't that she minded talking to Jacob; not at all. It was just that the waterfront was not her favorite place to be. All those men staring at her and making their crude remarks, not to mention the smell of the place. And then there was the time she had caught her heel and fallen headlong into that pile of crates. . . She felt her face burn at the remembrance.

But a promise was a promise, and that's what she had given to little Anna Peters—a promise. Not that it would matter very much since Raine would be gone soon, but still. . .

She realized she was almost running to keep up with the pace of her thoughts. Slowing her steps as well as her mind, she sighed, her mind replaying once again the meeting with the Mission's new administrator.

"I've only been here a couple of weeks, Miss Thomas," Mr. Duncan had begun in his frigid tone, "but already I can see that I do not approve of your methods for running the Mission school. They are not at all consistent with the rest of our efforts. Your informal attitude with your students encourages a laxness that I cannot condone."

Raine felt the blood rush into her face. "Mr. Duncan, I. . ."

"Please allow me to finish what I was saying, Miss Thomas."

Raine bit her tongue, feeling her world crumble around her as he finished his speech.

The rest of the painful conversation had dimmed in her memory, but the import of it had not. What it had come down to was that Mr. Duncan and his new advisory board felt strongly that a man would be more "suitable" as director of the Mission School. Raine was dismissed as of the end of the month.

But where can I go? She rubbed her hand over her forehead wearily. There was no use going over it again. Going home to Papa was out of the question, and she had already considered every other possible alternative. She drew a deep breath, wishing God would send her some kind of message, some guidance. The breath of air made her nose wrinkle; the air here by the wharf was heavy with moisture, making the ever-present odors of unwashed bodies and fresh fish almost unbearable.

I hope You're not calling me to be a fisherman, Lord. She smiled with a glimmer of her usual good humor. *I know You must have something for me. I just wish You'd show me what it is. . .*

Ah, there's Jacob. Raine's prayers were interrupted as she spotted the man she had been seeking. "Good morning, Jacob!" she called to the big fisherman.

"Miz Thomas," Jacob acknowledged, turning back to his nets after a brief nod in her direction.

"Your children haven't been to the Mission School in two weeks." Raine's tone was gentle, questioning. "Anna would like. . ."

"They're needed at home!" he growled. "Got to git back to work, Miz Thomas."

Raine sighed in aggravation as she turned to go. What would she tell Anna? She pictured the girl's sad little face. *I don't know why I even try anymore, when I'm going to be replaced in a few weeks anyway,* she thought, feeling a new wave of frustration and anger begin to flood over her. The now-familiar sick feeling in her stomach grew as she turned to go. *Lord, please give me strength. . .*

As she picked her way absently through the bustling wharf, she suddenly felt the weight of someone's gaze. Glancing around, she met a pair of bright blue eyes. The tall owner of the eyes took a step toward her, then turned on his heel and disappeared into the doorway where he had been standing.

Raine was not unaccustomed to admiring glances from strangers, but this was. . .different. *Almost as if he had wished to speak to me,* she thought. She shrugged off the odd sensation, focusing on making it to the street without catching her heel between the rotting boards of the wharf.

She breathed a sigh of relief as she reached the brick-paved street. So what was she going to do? It was already the fifteenth of the month, and she was no closer to finding somewhere else to go. *I'd sooner be a fisherman than go home,* she thought, recalling her prayer of a few minutes ago.

The Mission had been her home and employment for years now, and she hated to think of doing anything else besides teaching. True, some women did go to work in offices now. Perhaps she could even learn how to operate that queer new invention called a typewriter. *But I don't want to leave,* she thought. She loved teaching, and besides, what would become of the children? Their small faces had been so woebegone when she announced that she would be leaving.

"Why, Miss Thomas?"

"Don't ya love us no more?"

"Where're you going to go?"

The questions had nearly broken her heart. But she did have two more weeks. During that time, she would make sure they knew she loved them. And of course Charlotte would still be there for them. She just wasn't so sure about Mr. Graysdon, the new headmaster. She hoped he wouldn't be as stiff as he seemed. She sighed again. Life could be so. . .bothersome sometimes.

Her hat pins were poking unbearably by the time she neared the Mission. Yanking them out of her hat, she almost laughed with relief as she pulled the abominable thing off. Why did such large hats have to be in style these days anyway? Feeling decidedly grumpy and still no closer to a solution, she was looking forward to a time of quiet before she had to teach her afternoon class.

A crack of thunder hurried her toward the dilapidated steps of the old brownstone building. Hearing someone approaching from behind, she hastily jammed her hat back on. *I might as well at least try to stay in Mr. Duncan's good graces while*

I'm still here, she thought wryly. Mr. Duncan would be appalled to see his headmistress in public without her hat.

"Miss?"

Raine glanced back over her shoulder as she reached the top of the steps. The man from the wharf! Had he followed her here? She grasped the porch railing, turning to watch him jog up the steps to join her. His blue eyes searching her face, he stopped directly in front of her. Close. Close enough for her to see the vein pulsing in his neck.

&

Ben ran his fingers through his hair, feeling as if he were in a dream. It had to be her. His senses throbbed as he stood near enough to smell the lilac fragrance she wore. She was even more beautiful up close. . .

"Can I help you?" her tone was cool, interrupting his thoughts.

"Yes, I. . .ah. . ." Ben felt idiotic, but he had to know for sure. "My name is Ben Thackeray and I. . .could you take your hat off again?"

"What?"

"Please?" He tried to put his earnestness and uncertainty into his face, hoping she wouldn't deny his request. Reluctantly, she swept off her hat, cocking a questioning eyebrow at him.

There it was.

Ben sucked in his breath when he saw what he had suspected. The oddly shaped birthmark on her right temple seemed to jump out at him.

Her hand flew up of its own accord to cover the mark. She stared at him, her eyes wide. He came back to his senses then, realizing that he had frightened her. *You're such a cad,* he berated himself silently. *Couldn't you have been a little more subtle?*

"I'm sorry to appear so rude." He started to run his fingers through his sun-bleached hair, then stopped himself. He hadn't felt this nervous the first time he piloted the ship. The way she was staring at him didn't help matters any, either. He didn't like the wariness that lurked in her sage green eyes, as if he might actually harm her. She reminded him of a fawn he had startled out of its hiding spot once as he hiked through the woods.

"I'm sorry I frightened you," he apologized again. "I just had to be sure it was you. You are Raine Thomas. . .?"

Her face turned paler, if that were possible. She stood poised as if to run, just like the little deer. He grimaced. This wasn't exactly how he had pictured this moment happening. . . Not trusting himself to try to explain further, he drew a small package from his breast pocket. He unwrapped it with care and handed her the contents, watching carefully as she took the locket and held it to her heart.

"Paul?" she whispered.

He nodded.

She stared at him, her eyes begging him to give her hope. "Is he—alive?" Her voice was a tortured whisper.

He watched her compassionately, warring with himself. He longed to tell her what she wanted to hear, but. . . "Raine— may I call you that?"

She nodded.

"Let me tell you the story, then if you have any questions, I'll try to answer them as best I can. I'll start by saying that I don't know for sure that Paul is dead."

"Go on." Her voice trembled.

"I first met Paul in 1901, and. . ."

Raine interrupted, "1901. . .that was a year after he left. . .I was nineteen."

". . .and that's when he signed on as a crewman on one of my ships," Ben said. "I own a shipping company," he explained.

Raine smiled, as though the picture of Paul on a ship, his black hair glinting in the sun, a gentle breeze blowing, had broken through her anxiety. "He always did love to be on the water," she murmured lovingly. Her gaze grew misty and far-away.

"Raine?"

"I'm sorry. I was just. . ."

He smiled gently. "It's all right. I know this has all come as a shock to you." He saw her swallow a lump in her throat, and he looked away, giving her a chance to compose herself.

"How did you happen to have the locket?" Her voice still quavered.

"Paul and I had become quite close friends. He made me swear that if he ever needed me to, I would find you and give it to you." Ben's voice was rough with emotion. "I've been looking for you for three years, Raine."

"Three years!" Tears gathered in her eyes. "You haven't seen Paul in three years?"

Ben shook his head. "I'm sorry."

"Tell me the rest, please." She closed her eyes for a moment, as though she were dreading to hear what he would say next.

"There's not much more," he said slowly, hating to kill whatever hope she had left. "We pulled out from Boston on February 22, 1903. Since we primarily ship cargo, we didn't have too many passengers, thank God. There was a slight mishap as we left the harbor, but no one paid too much attention. The voyage went smoothly for the first week. . ." Ben stopped, unwilling to relive once again the horror of that night. It had been so cold, so quick, so. . .

He felt a small hand touch his lightly. "You can tell me," she encouraged him.

He drew a deep breath. "On Monday the twenty-eighth, I had just retired for the evening. Shortly after I got to bed, the warning alarms rang. I jumped up and raised the alarm. I banged on Paul's door," he remembered. "Fire was raging in the hold, and we soon realized we weren't going to be able to save the ship. We concentrated on getting the passengers into the lifeboats. Paul gave me the locket—he must have sensed . . .something." He shook his head. "The. . .the last I saw of Paul, he was helping a woman and her baby into lifeboat #4." Ben closed his eyes in pain, then went on. "We both had life jackets on, but there was so much confusion, and everything happened so fast. . . I was helping keep control of the situation on deck, and I just never saw Paul after that." He stopped abruptly, as if drained of all emotion.

Tears had been flowing down Raine's face as he talked. He gave her a wan smile, then standing up heavily, he offered her his hand. "I'm sorry, Raine," he whispered. "Most of the crew were able to get on the lifeboats. Some of the others were rescued from the water, but no one knows what happened to Paul. His body was never recovered." His hand rested on her shoulder for a brief moment, but his blue eyes never met hers again. "I'll be at my office tomorrow if you need to ask me anything more."

He handed her a card with the address elegantly inscribed on it, then turned and walked away.

≈

Raine stared after him a moment, then looked at the locket she still held clenched in her hand. "Where are you, Paul?" she whispered.

She stood rooted to the spot until the first cold drops of rain mingled with the warmth of her tears. Making her way slowly to her room, she ran into her friend Charlotte.

"Oh, Raine! I was just looking for you. Would you mind if I borrowed. . . What's the matter?"

"I'm not exactly sure, Charlotte." Raine gazed into the concerned eyes of her best friend. "Could you teach my class for me this afternoon?"

Charlotte nodded, giving Raine's shoulders a quick squeeze. "I'll pray for you."

Raine sank down on the bed remembering the day Paul had left. She had pressed the locket she always wore into his hand, needing to give him a part of herself to take with him. . .

She felt the pain stab her heart anew, and slipped to her knees, calling out to her only strength. *Father, please help me. I love Paul so much, and I always thought one day I would find him again. I need Your peace.* She stayed on her knees, a tiny flame of hope flickering in her heart. *The man did say that he didn't know for sure that Paul is dead,* she told herself. *But then why haven't you heard from him in so many years?*

She pushed that thought out of her mind, concentrating instead on the person who had brought her the news. What was his name? Ben something or other, she recalled. Tall and golden, he was the perfect counterpart to dark-haired, compactly-built Paul. *What a pair they must have been. They had to have been close friends for Paul to entrust Ben with the locket,* she mused.

The locket! Why hadn't she opened it before now? Maybe there was a message from Paul! Almost dropping it in her haste, she finally got the small heart open. Something white fell to the floor, so minute she might have missed it had she not seen it fall. She picked it up, unfolding the tiny piece of paper with trembling fingers.

Her heart began to pound as she recognized Paul's firm handwriting. Even in her agitation, she smiled to see that he had written in code. How like him. Racking her brain to remember the ciphers she had not used in years, she experimented for several minutes. It was just a simple substitution cipher; she was sure of it. She frowned in concentration, then smiled as it suddenly came to her. She decoded all that was legible, disappointed to find that most of the message was obliterated by waterstains.

Would Ben know what the missing words were? Could she trust him? *Surely if Paul trusted him with the locket, I can trust him with the message,* she decided, remembering his gentle eyes.

❧

Engrossed in his work, Ben started when he realized he was not alone in the office. He caught his breath when he saw Raine standing just inside the door, smiling at him uncertainly. *How lovely she is,* he thought, taking in the eager face and demure dress. Her dark curls were piled on top of her head today in the fashionable Gibson girl style. He was glad she wasn't wearing a hat, and wondered briefly what her hair would look like flowing around her face and down her back.

"How are you, Raine?" Ben rose to offer her a seat. He caught a whiff of her perfume and forced himself to sit down behind his desk.

"Quite well, thank you," she said. "Ben," she began, then

stopped, as though suddenly shy.

"What is it, Raine? Did you come up with some questions?" He was charmed with the way she held her chin down the tiniest bit, looking up at him.

"Yes, I. . . Did you know what was in the locket?"

He shook his head, saying nothing.

She looked at him thoughtfully. "Ben, how well did you know Paul?"

"He was my first mate and friend for two years." He looked into her eyes and saw the confusion there. "You can trust me, Raine," Ben said. "Paul was like a brother to me."

She stared at him for a long moment, then silently she pulled the water-stained note from her pocket and handed it to him. He stiffened as he stared at the strange writing. So, it was true all along. He wouldn't have believed it of Paul, but this proved it now, didn't it?

Raine's laughter broke into his glum thoughts. "I take it Paul didn't teach you any ciphers. I would have thought in all your time together, he would have shared his great passion with you."

She didn't seem to notice Ben's lack of response as she retrieved the note from him. "As you can see, the words near the bottom are missing. I was hoping you could help me fill in the gaps." She looked up at him appealingly. "What I have so far doesn't make much sense to me, but maybe you'll understand it: 'Am being pursued. Go to 284 H. . . Ask. . . key. I will be. . .going. . . C. . . Love, P.' "

Ben recovered himself quickly. Either Raine was an innocent party, or she played her part extremely well. He'd just play along for awhile and see what happened.

"Let's see. . . Go to 284 H. . .284. . .284. . . Sounds like an address," he muttered. "Wait a minute!" Whirling around to his file cabinet, he dug through it a moment, then triumphantly pulled out a sheet of paper. "This is a list of our crewmen's home addresses," he explained. "Ah, here it is! 284 High Street! Paul lived at 284 High Street in Boston!"

Raine jumped up from her chair with a shriek of joy. "But

what does the rest of the message mean?" she asked, returning his wide smile.

"I don't know, Raine," he said, sobering. "But at least you have a good start. I'll. . ."

"Mr. Thackeray, Miss Daniels is. . . Oh, excuse me." Ben's clerk backed out the door in confusion as he saw Raine.

"That's fine, Jerry. I'll be there in a moment," Ben called to the retreating clerk.

"Anyway, Raine, I'll think about the message and see if I can come up with anything else. Can you come back to the office in the morning?"

"Certainly," Raine said crisply, a hint of annoyance in her tone.

"I'll be looking forward to it, Raine Ellen." Ben's voice was soft.

After she left, he leaned back in his chair, a small smile playing about his lips. The look that had crossed Raine's face when Miss Daniels had been announced had been priceless. Nevertheless, he was loathe to face the consequences of keeping one Vida Daniels waiting, so he had unwillingly hurried Paul's lovely fiancée on her way.

Watching her out the window now as he rose to admit Miss Daniels, Ben was startled as he glimpsed a large, red-haired man standing in the shadows of a the tavern next door. The man watched Raine until she disappeared from view, then turned and stared intently at Ben's office. Apparently satisfied, he sauntered onto the busy wharf and was swallowed up in the crowd.

Something about the man seemed familiar to Ben, but he couldn't be sure. He would have given it more thought, but the insistent tapping on his office door grew unavoidable. Rolling his eyes in aggravation, he opened the door to a very red-faced Miss Daniels, narrowly missing being jabbed by the end of her parasol as she pushed past him into the room.

"Good morning, Miss Daniels," Ben said as politely as possible. "I was just coming out to greet you. Won't you have a chair?" *A chair in another country would do nicely,* he thought.

Her irritation inexplicably erased by the warm smile Ben had given her as she left his office, Raine had smiled at Ben in return and then, hoping to get a glimpse of Miss Daniels, she took her time in passing through the outer office. But besides the clerk Jerry who studiously avoided looking her way, the only others present were two elderly women. Neither of them could possibly be Miss Daniels, she surmised disappointedly.

Strolling back to the Mission, she pondered what her next step should be. *Is this Your doing, Father?* she prayed. The tiny seed of desire to go to America had been planted long ago, but had never sprouted until today. *Am I to go to Boston? Please show me Your will, Lord.*

Something was tugging at the back of her mind, causing her to lose her train of thought. She glanced behind her several times, feeling as though she were being watched. Unable to catch a glimpse of anyone, she shrugged the feeling aside as she entered the Mission building. The familiar smell of ancient books, unwashed children, and stewed onions was somehow comforting, and her little room felt cool after the hot mid-morning sun. She knelt by her bed, suddenly feeling full of unexplained anticipation. Picking up her Bible, she began reading where she had left off last night. *And I will bring the blind by a way that they knew not; I will lead them in paths that they have not know: I will make darkness light before them. . .* The verse from Isaiah leapt out at her, filling her heart with the peace that she needed. The Bible was talking about her life, she realized. "I need You to lead me," she whispered. "I can't see where I'm going and I will be walking some unfamiliar paths. . ."

By the next morning, the tiny sprout of desire to go to America had bloomed into a magnificent flower. She had resolved one thing—she was going to Boston! The last she had heard from Paul, he had been in Boston. And now the message in the locket. She was sure it was not a coincidence.

I'll find you, Paul, she vowed. *By God's grace I'll find you.*

Convinced that Ben could help her, Raine rehearsed her request as she dressed. Surely such a close friend of Paul's would be willing to give her a little advice, wouldn't he? Even if he wouldn't agree to help her, she'd get to Boston somehow. *I know You're leading me there, Lord.* She brushed her long, dark hair until it shone, then made a face at herself in the mirror. *Just who are you trying to impress, Raine Thomas?* She laughed out loud, her heart light. It felt so good to be happy again.

Twisting her hair into a loose chignon, she chose her favorite hat. More comfortable than the rest of the hats she owned, the small cream-colored toque was trimmed with navy velvet. It was perfect with her favorite shirt-waist suit.

She took one last peek in the mirror and closed the door firmly behind her. Her hurried descent down the stairs was anything but ladylike, so it was with some dismay that she found Mr. Duncan waiting for her at the foot of the stairway.

"Good day, Miss Thomas." He nodded politely, obviously choosing to ignore her breach of conduct. "I haven't seen much of you lately. Have you had any success in finding a new. . .ah, position?"

"I just may have, Mr. Duncan." She tried hard not to smile at the expression on his face. She always imagined he must have perpetual stomach acid or some other malady to make him frown so.

"Humph." He shook his head as she yielded to the temptation to smile. Her smile broadened as she sailed out the door.

❧

Pushing through the door that read "Thackeray Shipping Co.," Raine nearly ran headlong into Jerry, who seemed to be embarrassed to be caught combing the few strands of hair he had left on his head.

"Pardon me, Jerry," she apologized to the clerk. "Is Mr. Thackeray in yet this morning?"

"Not until nine." He cocked his head, reminding her of a large parrot she had seen once at the fair.

She looked at the clock. Ten minutes till nine. She sat down, then stood up, too excited to sit still. Pacing around the little office, the many drawings and photographs that cluttered the walls caught her eye. She stopped in front of a grouping of framed sketches depicting various ships. The *Ladyhawk,* the *Golden Hind,* the *Half Moon,* the *Goodspeed,* the *Constellation.* What romantic names these ships bore. Maybe Paul had sailed on one of these.

She could almost see him standing on the deck, wearing a smart blue uniform. A smile creased his face while the wind ruffled his coal-black hair. . .

"Good morning, Miss Thomas."

She whirled around. "Mr. Thackeray! You startled me!"

His twinkling blue eyes held the same look as six-year-old Tim's had the day he had put a frog in her desk drawer. "Please, call me Ben. May I escort you into my office?" He pulled out a chair for Raine. "Now, tell me what that sparkle in your eye means."

"I'm going to America!" Ben's eyebrows shot up, but he said nothing as she continued. "I've been saving my money for a long time so I could start searching for Paul. The last time I heard from him, he was in Boston, and the address in the locket just confirms that I should begin searching there," she explained logically. Her green eyes shone with determination. "If Paul is alive, I will find him."

Ben's eyes lingered on her face, his expression almost wistful. He said, "It sounds as if you've pretty much made up your mind, Raine. How do you plan on getting there?"

"Well, I. . ."

"You aren't planning to go alone?" he interrupted, suddenly remembering the man he had seen watching her earlier.

"Well, yes, I. . ."

"Do you know how dangerous New York can be, let alone the journey over there?" He was incredulous. "Besides, you'd never make it in without a sponsor."

"Ben," Raine said quietly. "I'm not afraid, and I do have a place to stay once I get there. My Uncle John who lives in Boston has offered over and over to sponsor me." She hesitated, and then said, "I was hoping you could recommend a reputable ship. I've heard the horror stories. . ."

Ben nodded. He had seen some of the wretched vessels firsthand. He would never put his worst enemy aboard such a ship, if they could be called ships. He stared out the window, an idea forming slowly. "How long would it take you to get your papers in order?" he asked finally.

"I was hoping to leave within the month."

"Hmm."

She waited.

At last he said, "Yes, I think that will work out perfectly."

"I beg your pardon?"

"Simple." He grinned at her. "You can go with me as far as New York, then I'll escort you the rest of the way to. . . Where did you say you were going to stay?"

Raine shook her head. "What do you mean, go with you?" She stared at him.

"You can lower your eyebrows, Miss Thomas. I'm not suggesting anything improper." He chuckled at the blush that rose to her cheeks. "You know that we don't take many passengers on our ships." He paused until she nodded. "But I was planning to go to New York this month to take care of some business anyway. I would be glad for the pleasure of your company."

"On one of your cargo ships?" she asked, considering the plan.

"Yes." He made a face. "It's not as luxurious as a passenger ship, of course, but you would have your own cabin, and the food is decent. Oh, and there will be several other women aboard," he added, putting to rest her last fear.

She eyed him thoughtfully. Could she trust this man? It was hard to believe she was actually considering going halfway across the world, much less with a man she hardly knew. What would Papa think? And what if Ben weren't as trustworthy as he seemed? What if. . . Suddenly the peace that she had felt after her prayer the day before came flooding over her again.

"When do we leave?"

"The *Capernaum* departs in sixteen days. Can you be ready?"

"The *Capernaum*?"

A strange look dropped into Ben's eyes. "All my ships are named after Biblical cities. I'm not sure why, actually. I suppose it's a habit I picked up from my father." He cleared his throat. "Can you be ready to go by then?"

"I'll be ready. How much will I owe you?"

He looked at her blankly. "Owe me? Oh, for the passage. Let's just say it's a favor to an old friend."

Raine was overwhelmed. She had been wondering if the small amount she had managed to save over the last few years would be enough. "Thank you," she whispered, sudden tears threatening to spill over.

He stepped closer to her and said softly, "Paul was more than just a first mate, he was my friend. It's the least I can do."

She gave him a small smile, and she saw his eyes widen, his lips part—and then he took a quick step backward and said brusquely, "Now—I'm sure you have a lot of things to attend to before we depart, and I need to get busy with this paperwork." He moved back another step away from her. "I'll call on you sometime next week to make arrangements for the voyage."

Raine blinked at the abrupt change in mood, then turned to leave. "I'll be ready," she said softly. He didn't look up from his desk.

❧

Ben rose to stand at the window as soon as the door closed behind her. He stared after her, wanting nothing more than to run after her. Even the photograph of her he had fallen in love with years ago didn't do justice to her beauty.

I could almost wish she would never find Paul. . . He turned away sharply. *Get ahold of yourself, Thackeray,* he told himself. *Her heart will always belong to Paul.*

❧

Unaware of the turmoil she was causing Ben, Raine made her way home to the Mission with a light step. Feeling as though an enormous weight had been lifted from her shoulders, she dipped herself a glass of ice cold water from the bucket in the kitchen, then went directly to Mr. Duncan's office. Her knock was firm.

"Come."

Raine entered the stuffy office and immediately began to recite the speech she had practiced on the way. ". . .and so, I'll be departing in approximately two weeks."

"Well, this is a surprise." He sniffed. "I suppose you've made proper arrangements for your, ah, excursion?"

She was slightly ashamed of herself for enjoying his reaction to her news. "Yes, sir. I will be traveling on a reputable ship, and I already have a sponsor in America."

"Your duty to the Mission does not expire until the end of the month, Miss Thomas," Mr. Duncan reminded her. "I expect you to fulfill your obligation."

She sighed in frustration. She had thought he would be happy to be rid of her. "Mr. Graysdon has already arrived to take my place, has he not?"

"Yes, he has."

"I sincerely doubt that one extra day will be a burden on him," Raine said, hoping she sounded more polite than she felt.

"I will not tolerate impertinence, Miss Thomas," he snapped. "If you insist on leaving on the thirtieth, I will subtract two days' wages from your salary."

She gritted her teeth. Why did this man remind her so much of Papa? Sending up a silent prayer for patience, she restrained herself from dumping the glass of water down his back. Forcing her voice to stay calm, she looked him in the eye. "I'm sorry you feel that way, Mr. Duncan, but I don't have much of a choice. I have to be on that ship when it sails."

His raised eyebrows were his only response.

She fled from his office, convinced that her tongue would get her in trouble if she lingered one more second. *That is one person I certainly won't miss,* Raine thought uncharitably as she climbed the stairs to her room, unsure if she were referring to Papa or Mr. Duncan. Her conscience pricked her. *And aren't you a sweet one today,* she thought uncomfortably.

❧

Three days later she looked up from her desk to see Ben grinning at her from the back of the classroom. Startled, she dropped her eyes back down to the tests she was grading. What was he doing here?

"All right, children. You may open your readers now. We will begin on page forty-two." She sincerely hoped she had remembered to powder her nose before class. If not, it was surely shining like one of those electric light bulbs she had heard about. "James, start reading aloud please."

She went to greet her visitor. "Ben. How nice to see you." All at once there didn't seem to be enough air to breathe.

"And you." He was silent then, leaning against the door-jamb comfortably. He studied her face like it was the morning newspaper. It made her nervous.

"Can I help you?" The same words she used the first time they met. She felt herself color.

A smile crept into his eyes and twitched at the corner of his mouth. "I just came by to see if we could have supper together this evening, say, around six o'clock? I need go over the details of the voyage with you."

"Oh yes, the voyage." He wasn't staring at her nose, was he?

"You haven't changed your mind?"

"No. I, ah. . ." Raine noticed her students had stopped reading and were gawking. "Six o'clock would be fine."

His parting smile was enough to turn the rest of her day upside down.

❧

"You're going to supper with the captain of the ship?" Charlotte's brown eyes were huge. "Is he the one who brought you the locket from Paul?"

"Mmm-hmm." Raine answered around a mouthful of hair-pins.

"Tsk, tsk. What would Paul say?"

"There." Raine stuck the last pin in and tilted her head to see the side of her hair. "Paul wouldn't say anything. It's just a business meeting."

"Ah." Charlotte nodded. "Then why are you taking so many pains?"

Raine glared at her friend as she fastened the lacy guimpe around her neck. "Speaking of pains. . ."

Charlotte laughed. "All right, I'll leave you alone. But do I at least get to meet him?"

❧

"Ben, this is my good friend, Charlotte Denoire. Charlotte, Captain Ben Thackeray." Raine rolled her eyes as Charlotte curtsied. She noticed her friend had added a bit of extra lip rouge for the occasion.

"A pleasure I'm sure, Miss Denoire." Ben bent over her outstretched hand for the briefest second. He turned to Raine. "Shall we?"

She smiled up at him as he took her arm, the glint of humor in his eye doing wonders for her disposition.

Big Ben was booming out the hour of seven by the time they reached the Golden Cross Hotel.

"Oh, I've always wanted to eat here." Her mouth began to water at the aromas wafting from the famous establishment.

He smiled at her. "Are you hungry?"

"As a horse."

Ben laughed out loud.

❧

El Paso County, Colorado

Tom Cox sat astride his panting mount, surveying with pride the land spread before him. He absently rubbed the scar on his left cheek as he gazed with appreciation at the majestic Rocky Mountains looming blue and mysterious in the distance. Though it appeared one could reach the cool shade of the Rockies in a matter of minutes, he knew from experience that the ride was long and dusty. Wistfully, he turned once again to the east, shielding his dark eyes from the glare of the newly-risen sun.

He owns the cattle on a thousand hills. The bit of Scripture came unbidden to his mind as he gazed upon the gently rolling plains and grazing cattle that comprised the Crooked P Ranch. Frowning in annoyance at his train of thought, he urged the patient mare forward.

"Come on, Trixie. Let's go home." Slouching comfortably in the saddle, he let the horse pick her way home through the sagebrush as he reflected on the past couple of years. The young Denver City had been more progressive than he had expected it to be, but the "Queen City of the Plains" nonetheless still carried with it the unmistakable influences of the wild west. Everywhere he looked were Stetson hats and cowboy boots; feed stores and saloons shared the street with banks and lawyer's offices.

Glad that he was going to be some distance from the city's hustle and bustle, Tom had wasted no time in obtaining a horse. Riding southward past Colorado Springs to the land he had purchased sight-unseen, he was awestruck by the wild beauty of the land, grateful that he had chosen this place to start anew. Now, three years later, the Crooked P Ranch was prospering.

Trixie picked up her pace as they passed the bunkhouse and neared the stable. Her rider dismounted with a troubled sigh. He had made a home in this untamed, yet peaceful land. His ranch was prospering, but his soul was not. There remained a chapter in his life he could not close. . .

two

Up since three A.M., Raine was awaiting Ben's arrival, feeling much the same as she did the morning of her first day of school. The stillness of the gray, pre-dawn hours contrasted sharply with the butterflies dancing in her midsection.

As she made her way downstairs, no one else in the Mission stirred; she had said all of her good-byes yesterday. The surprise party for the children had gone so well. She knew she would never forget the joy in their eyes as they opened the tiny gifts she had managed to get for each one. Nor would she forget the arms wrapped around her neck and the shy kisses placed on her cheek. It was harder than she had thought to be leaving them, and she wasn't even gone yet! Equally hard was ignoring the tiny pricks of guilt she felt when she thought of her decision to leave without telling Papa good-bye.

After peering out the window yet again, she dropped down in the straight-backed chair in the Mission's front parlor. Her Bible was lying on top of her carpetbag. She picked it up and began to read until a soft knock on the door alerted her to Ben's arrival.

"Good morning!" His eyes studied her face, and she was sure he saw the excitement that radiated from her heart.

"Good morning to you!"

She saw his gaze drop to her mouth for the briefest instant before he said firmly, "We'd better get going." His tone was tight as he gathered her luggage and directed her out the front door.

She glanced at him as he preceded her, carrying her trunk. Had she done something wrong, for him to become so brusque all the sudden? Or perhaps he was regretting taking her along? "Ben."

He looked up from loading her baggage into the carriage.

"Are you sure you want to take me to Boston?" she ventured in a small voice.

"Of course I want you to go," he said a little too heartily. "Don't mind me. I've got a lot on my mind this morning." He didn't meet her eyes.

Raine frowned, studying his face, but her thoughts were interrupted by a voice behind her.

"Raine! I'm so glad I caught you before you left!" A sleepy-eyed Charlotte came flying down the front steps, her mousy hair still in braids.

Raine smiled at her friend. "I haven't even left yet, and you miss me so much already?"

"No. I mean, yes. Oh, you know what I mean." Charlotte reached behind her back and pressed a soft package into Raine's hand. "I'll miss you, Raine."

Tears filled Raine's eyes. "I'll miss you, too, Char. I'll pray for you."

"And I you."

They gazed at one another. "Don't forget to write to me, Charlotte."

"Maybe I'll come and join you in America sometime."

"I'll look for the day."

With a last hug, they said good-bye and Raine climbed into the carriage. Although tears still clouded her vision, Raine's anticipation grew as she caught glimpses of the waterfront through the early morning fog. Sensing Ben's reticence, she had refrained from chattering on the short drive, but now she couldn't help it.

"The *Capernaum* is so much larger than I expected," she commented, gazing at the huge ship.

"Yes, she's a hefty one," Ben replied, following Raine's gaze. "There's no telling how many storms she's weathered, but she hums along like it was her maiden voyage," he added proudly.

The lonely cries of gulls and a damp, fishy smell assailed her senses as Ben assisted her out of the carriage. There seemed to be barrels and crates everywhere, not to mention the baggage of the passengers and crew. Ben gave her his arm and they waded through what seemed to be mountains of rope to get to the gangway. *Thank goodness bustles have gone out of fashion,* she thought. *It would have been almost impossible to dodge these barrels of pickled herring while wearing one of those ridiculous things.*

"Mornin' Cap'n; Miss." A bewhiskered sailor nodded to Ben and Raine, then leaned down to grasp Raine's small trunk.

Looking up at Ben, Raine said lightly, "Shall I call you 'sir' from now on, now that I'm on your ship?"

"No," he said. "You're not a part of the crew, you're. . .a friend," he finished, his blue gaze holding her captive.

Raine stared back at him, seeing him as if for the first time. She clasped her hands together behind her back, quelling an unexpected desire to run her fingers through his golden brown hair.

"Miss."

Raine jumped. The grizzled sailor was holding her last bag, studying her with a curious expression. "Are you ready to go aboard?"

"Ah. . .yes. That would be fine." She turned. "I'll be seeing you later, Captain?"

"Yes, perhaps tomorrow, Miss Thomas." He hated his formal tone, but he couldn't seem to help himself. "Sully here will get you settled in and answer any questions you might have."

I'm sure Sully can answer any question I have except the question of why you act so strangely sometimes, Ben Thackeray, she thought, still shaken by the intensity of his gaze. Obediently following the patient Sully, she turned to wave to Ben, but he was gone.

⁂

Settled at last in her small but adequate cabin, Raine took in a breath of cool air that was blowing in through the open port-hole. The butterflies in her stomach had settled down to a slow waltz.

She opened the small package from Charlotte, shaking

her head as she read the note that accompanied the hand-embroidered pillowcase set.

Dear Raine,
These are for your new home in America. I hope
you'll remember me when you see them and pray that
God sends me as handsome a man as He sent you.
Love and prayers,
Charlotte

Poor Char. She was only biding her time until a handsome prince came to sweep her off her feet. To her, teaching was just a way of making a living. To Raine, it was a life's calling.

Feeling her throat tighten, she pushed thoughts of the children from her mind. God was leading her away from the Mission, and she would not allow herself to wallow in misery. Of course she would miss the children, but God had something better for her, didn't He? He would have something better for the children too.

Of course He would, she assured herself as she powdered her nose. God was definitely leading her forward, and all she had to do was follow, no matter how unfamiliar the way seemed. The first step would be to find Paul. That in itself would be a glorious thing. She brushed her teeth with enthusiasm, picturing the moment. First he would stare at her in disbelief. . .then he would open his arms. . .

When she felt the ship lurch, she flew up to the top deck, not wanting to miss any of the action. After all, it was her first time out to sea. Watching with interest as the men worked to set the huge ship into motion, she could readily imagine Paul doing such work. She scanned the deck and was not surprised to see Ben working alongside his crew, clad in the clothes of a deckhand. He looked dashing.

Finally, a cheer went up as the *Capernaum* slowly maneuvered her way out of the harbor. The voyage was underway! "I'm coming, Paul!" she whispered. A quick prayer of thanksgiving flowed from her heart as the gulls dipped and swooped their farewells. *Hang on, love. I'm coming.*

≈

Ben was fuming. Angry with himself for giving in to his feelings, he was even angrier at Raine. *How can she look at me like that when she's engaged to Paul?* He paced up and down in his spacious cabin. *I never should have offered to let her come on this ship. I'll just stay away from her as much as possible, then get her to Boston quickly,* he vowed to himself.

He soon realized that it was not going to be easy to avoid the lovely Raine Thomas. Having made arrangements for her and the six other paying passengers to take their meals with him and his officers, he knew he couldn't shun her without drawing censure from the rest of the company.

At dinner that night, he watched as she chatted away with the buxom woman next to her. What was her name? Oh, yes. Constance. Constance Rabinowicz.

He compared the two woman unconsciously. Raine in her traveling suit of navy blue, with that charming hat to set it off. Constance with her overly large hat and even larger bustle. Turning his attention back to Raine, he was mesmerized by the sound of her low voice. She glanced up then and their eyes locked.

"Who's the girl?" His first mate followed Ben's eyes.

"Miss Thomas is the fiancée of a friend."

"Oh?" Griff's eyebrows shot up. "He'd better marry her fast," he said mischievously, watching his captain out of the corner of his eye.

Ben glared at him. "Keep your observations to yourself, Griff."

≈

Ben stood at to the railing a few evenings later. Bowing his head, he stood gazing into the dark waters for a long time. He was so weary. Weary in body, yes; but had he only admitted it to himself, most of the weariness was in his soul. He was weary of his constant fight against fear, the fear of surrender.

He was losing the battle. He had managed to stay away from Raine except when it was impossible to do so. Aware of the wistful look in her eyes, he knew she was puzzled by his behavior. Now with only a few days left before they arrived in New York, he had yielded to his longing to seek her out. Turning, he followed the path she'd taken toward her cabin.

His hand poised to knock on her cabin door, he stopped as he heard her singing. At first impressed with her melodic voice, soon he was caught up in the words she was singing.

> "O the love that drew salvation's plan!
> O the grace that brought it down to man!
> O the mighty gulf that God did span at Calvary!
> Mercy there was great, and grace was free;
> Pardon there was multiplied to me;
> There my burdened soul found liberty
> At Calvary."

Slow tears began to course unheeded down his face. *God, how I long to know once again the peace that comes from accepting Your grace!* He had seen that same peace reflected so often in Raine's eyes. *But how can I?* his heart cried. *To whom much is given, much is required.* The fragment of Scripture that had been pounded into his mind as a child came back to hammer him once again. *God, I'm so afraid. I'm afraid of what You will require of me. . .*

Ben turned to go, to run from the familiar words of Raine's songs, but he could not run from the insistent, loving call of the Father. . .

❧

The sunny June days slipped by as the *Capernaum* steamed steadily toward New York. Raine had brought a couple of books with her, planning on catching up on her reading. However, that was not to be.

"Yoo hoo! Raine!"

She sighed, wishing not for the first time that Constance Rabinowicz had chosen another ship on which to immigrate to America. She didn't want to be unkind to the woman, but she did wish she could have just a few minutes of quiet to read. Maybe if she ignored her she would go away.

"Raine! Over here!" Constance increased her volume, further fortifying her presence by waving her handkerchief.

As if I were a cow being shooed into the barn, Raine thought. Grudgingly placing the marker in the volume of Tennyson, she rose. "I'm coming, Constance." She tried to wipe the frustration and annoyance from her face, but she couldn't wipe it from her heart. Constance seemed to want to spend every minute chatting with her, eating up the quiet, peaceful hours with her constant prattle.

She also had to resign herself to the fact that Ben was too busy to spend much time with her; he almost seemed to be avoiding her. *Perhaps he's just preoccupied,* she thought. Disappointed that she hadn't had a chance to talk with him more, she hoped they would have more time together on the trip from New York to Boston.

That night at dinner, she felt his eyes on her as she finished the last of her plum pudding. Glancing at him, she was surprised that he didn't look away, but held her gaze before turning to answer a question from one of the men. *He looks more relaxed tonight,* she thought as she studied him. *Perhaps he's glad that we're almost to New York.* She looked down at her plate. In truth, she too was glad that this leg of her journey was almost over. She was not accustomed to so much leisure time, and Constance was grating on her nerves. Besides, she was anxious to begin her search for Paul.

"Excuse me, Miss Thomas. May I take your plate?" The cabin boy's voice intruded on her thoughts. Glancing about, she realized almost everyone else had left the table, even Constance. Raine had heaved a sigh of relief earlier when she heard the older woman accept an invitation to play bridge with two of the other passengers. An evening to herself at last!

She gathered her skirts and turned, only to come face to face with Ben. He smiled at her startled look. "Would you care to take a turn around the deck, Raine?"

She raised her eyebrows.

"It's a beautiful night," he coaxed, offering her his arm.

She slipped her arm through his, watching him surreptitiously as they walked up the stairs to the deck. His hair had become bleached even lighter and his skin was a golden tan from the days spent working with the crew. She liked how the deep blue uniform he wore set off the blue of his eyes.

The slight breeze toyed with the curls around her face as they reached the deck. Ben tucked her arm in closer. "Lovely night, isn't it?"

By their third trip around the deck, the crew began to glance at them with ill-concealed curiosity. Raine felt her stomach begin to twist into knots. Finally, she could stand it no longer.

"Ben, was there something specific you wished to talk to me about?" she asked. Tactfulness had never been one of her strong points. She bit her lip, then went on. "It seems that you've been avoiding me, and I thought since you sought me out tonight, maybe you needed to tell me something important." She finished in a rush, confused by the expression in his eyes.

"Ah Raine," he sighed.

❧

Ben led her gently into the shadows, away from curious eyes. Leaning on the railing, he gazed out into the blackness. *Why am I torturing myself?* he thought. *After all these years of waiting for the right woman, and then I fall in love with one who belongs to someone else.* It had been fine when all he had was a photograph, but now that she was here beside him, gazing at him so seriously with those big emerald eyes. . .

He didn't trust himself to look at her for fear he would take her in his arms, yet he was unwilling to let her go from his presence. He asked her the first question that popped into his head, hoping to keep her near him a little longer. "Tell me about your family, Raine."

She threw him an odd look, he noticed, but apparently she decided to humor him.

"My papa is a preacher," she began. "Papa is a strong man, and not always easy to get along with. But I'm sure Paul told you all about that," she added wryly. "Anyway, Papa always. . ."

"Tell me about you and Paul." Ben interrupted her narrative, suddenly curious about their relationship.

She smiled, a faraway look coming into her eyes. "Well, it's hard to know where to begin. Paul always understood me like no one else. He. . ."

I really don't want to hear this, he thought. About to interrupt her again, he froze as he heard her next words.

". . .Papa always said I was the willful one in the family, but Paul was just as bad, really. He always did take my side, though. Once he even let Papa paddle him instead of me, even when I had been the one to. . ." Her sentence trailed off at the strange look on Ben's face.

An amazing thought had just occurred to him. *Please, God, let it be true!* Gripping her by the shoulders, he searched her face. "Raine." His voice sounded as if he hadn't used it in a hundred years. He cleared his throat. "Is Paul your brother?"

"Of course he's my brother!" she replied in amazement. "Surely you knew that?"

The look on his face answered her question. "I thought you were to be married," he said at last, hoping he didn't look as addled as he felt. "I knew Paul loved you. I just assumed. . . It never occurred to me. . ."

"I never dreamed you didn't know Paul and I are brother and sister, Ben. I'm sorry." Looking up at him now, she smiled, and he was certain that she must see the relief and joy on his face.

He grinned back at her, feeling ridiculously giddy. "This definitely sheds new light on the situation. I thought you were too beautiful for someone like that old scalawag brother of yours anyway."

"And just what is that supposed to mean?" Raine's voice was stern, but her eyes danced.

He merely smiled, letting her interpret his words as she would. "Come on, Raine, I'm starving. Let's go raid the galley."

Leaving her at the door of her cabin hours later, Ben touched her cheek gently. "Sleep well," he whispered.

❧

She closed the door behind him, then whirled around the room a few times before sinking into the nearest chair. What a wonderful evening! Closing her eyes, she could picture again the look in Ben's eyes when he had learned that Paul was not her intended. Could it be that he felt the same way about her as she was beginning to feel about him? She had already admitted to herself that she was attracted to Ben, but had tried hard to dismiss thoughts of him from her mind because. . .because why? She had never really thought about it before.

Because you don't want to end up like your mother. The thought shocked her. *But Ben is not the least bit like Papa. . . or is he?* She had to admit she had never seen Ben under pressure. Would he fly off the handle and blame everything on someone else, as Papa often did? She had watched her mother take the brunt of Papa's anger over the years, usually over something that didn't even have anything to do with her. And then there was the way Papa was away from home so much. Was Ben married to his work as Papa had been? Sea captains probably had to be gone often.

Good grief, Raine, she scolded herself. *You act like he asked you to marry him or something. And I thought he was regretting that he had offered to escort me to Boston,* she thought with a smile. Realizing now that he had been staying away from her because of loyalty to Paul made her admire him all the more.

After their conversation, they both realized they were hungry, since neither of them had eaten much at supper. They had giggled like guilty school children as they snooped around the galley. Ben cut them each a huge slice of dried-apple pie that was still slightly warm.

"I hope Cook wasn't saving this for a special occasion," Raine whispered as they smuggled their loot back up on deck.

"This is the most special occasion I've had in a long time, Raine," Ben said, gazing deep into her eyes.

She had blushed and almost choked on her pie. Even now

she could feel the heat flood her face as she thought of it.

"You're being silly, Raine Thomas," she scolded herself. Surely the evening didn't mean anything to him. Sighing, she wished for another piece of pie and a pair of sea-blue eyes to go with it. Instead came a knock on the door.

"Are you still awake, Raine?"

Even if I wasn't, I would be now, Raine groused to herself as she swung the door open. "Constance! What a surprise!" She stood back to allow the other woman to enter. Constance plopped down in a chair, looking eager for a long chat.

"So, what are you planning to do once you arrive in America, Constance?" Raine asked politely as the other woman settled herself more comfortably.

Constance pleated the folds of her skirt thoughtfully. "You know, I've wondered that myself."

"Oh?"

"Yes. I really didn't have much choice in the matter, you see."

Raine didn't see, but she nodded anyway.

"My husband. . .well, my family didn't approve of me marrying him. Although he was Jewish by birth, he'd long ago stopped practicing Judaism. In fact, he even attended a Christian church. I believe he did it for business reasons only, but my family refused to have anything more to do with me. In their minds, I am dead. I was so lonely, but I found comfort in the church we attended. I believed that Christ is the Messiah. . ."

She shrugged. "Well, my husband and I never had what you'd call a close marriage, but I threw myself into our church and filled my time that way. But then last year, my husband took up with some young thing and decided he didn't have any more use for me. He put me on this ship with a small fortune and wished me good luck in my new life." She turned her head in the pretense of brushing a speck of lint, but not before Raine saw the tears shimmering in her eyes.

"I'm very sorry to hear that, Constance." In truth, she felt like a heel. Had she been so wrapped up in her own little dream world that she'd become a snob? Surely she should have been able to see that the woman's overdone behavior sprang out of pain. *God, please forgive me,* she prayed silently.

Without meaning to, she yawned. "We need to get some sleep, Constance. But why don't you come to my cabin in the morning? My uncle John sent me some newspapers to read and maybe you could find some sort of work in there that you'd be able to do."

The smile on Constance's plump face erased a bit of Raine's regret.

She got ready for bed and slid between the covers, but hours later, she still hadn't been able to fall asleep, despite her tiredness. At last, she slipped from the narrow bed onto her knees, pouring out the evening's events to her heavenly Father.

Abruptly, Raine realized that she didn't know if Ben knew her Lord. *Oh Father,* she prayed earnestly, *please touch Ben. If he is not Yours, I pray that You would draw him to You. Please give me peace about my feelings toward him. . .*

&

The next day found Ben at his desk gazing vacantly at the dark porthole. Running his fingers through his hair, he leaned back with an exasperated sigh. *I have got to get this work done before we get to New York,* he thought.

He had been sitting here trying to work since early afternoon, but he was unable to get Raine off of his mind. Surely she was as innocent as she seemed. Her ready smile, the way her dark hair glinted in the sunlight. . .he shook his head. *You're never going to get anything done at this rate, old boy.* Finally he gave up and headed downstairs for supper.

Raine was already seated at the table. She flashed him a quick smile as he entered the room.

"Want to go for a walk after supper?" He leaned close enough that he knew she must feel his breath warm against her ear, and he didn't miss the quick blush that rose to her cheeks.

She nodded, her green eyes sparkling.

As he turned to take a seat, he saw Constance elbow her. "You and the Cap'n got somethin' goin'?"

Ben winced. As he began to eat, he had the feeling that the meal would never end. His impatience grew when Lloyd Ferris insisted on involving him in a conversation about Britain's recent agreement with China to limit the production of opium. It was a subject that normally interested Ben, but now the topic dragged on through the whole main course and dessert. From time to time, he cast apologetic glances in Raine's direction.

She smiled at him down the table. Finally free, Ben took her arm and once again escorted her up the stairs to the top deck. As if by mutual agreement, they walked to the same spot at the railing as the previous night. They stood gazing out over the soft waves for long moments, each wrapped in their own thoughts.

At last Raine turned. "I suppose I should finish the story I began telling you last night about Paul."

Ben smiled at her. "Maybe you should start at the beginning and tell me why Paul left home in the first place. He told me bits and pieces, but obviously I don't have the whole picture."

"Apparently not," she agreed. "Paul was always my best friend," she began thoughtfully. "He could always come up with something fun to do, and we often made up games that only the two of us knew how to play. One of our favorite games was to pretend we were spies. He made up all kinds of codes and ciphers, and we had to use them any time we wanted to send a message to each other."

The relief Ben felt was almost palpable. She was innocent, he was sure of it now. He silently blessed Paul for not involving her.

Raine's laugh was gentle, remembering. "We had so much fun. My friend Christina and her older brother Geoff Hathaway were our best friends, and sometimes we'd get them in on the game as well. We didn't really use the codes much after we all got older, but when Paul got in trouble. . ." Raine's words stopped as she recalled those painful days.

"Go on, Raine," he prompted gently.

"I told you before that my father is a preacher."

He nodded.

"Papa loved us deeply. He could be a lot of fun, but was very stern at times as well. He was the pastor of a good-sized church, and that kept him so busy, he was gone a lot of the time."

She was silent, remembering all the nights Papa's place at the supper table had been empty. "He is doing God's work," Raine's mother had said. Yet. . .

"It seems like it all started after Geoff found that old book of ciphers." She shook her head. "I never did know exactly what happened between Paul and Geoff, but their relationship was ruined. They argued. . . A few months later, Geoff died when the family's house burned down. It was horrible."

She closed her eyes for a moment. "Anyway, Paul started courting a beautiful girl named Lucinda right around that time. I was surprised, because he'd always been sweet on Christina. But Lucinda's family attended our church, and everyone seemed pleased with the match.

"Then quite abruptly, they stopped seeing each other. He would never tell me why." She sighed. "After that, Paul began spending more and more time with some boys he had gone to school with. They were a rough lot, and he began to pick up some of their ways. He spent a lot of time at the tavern. He wasn't bad, though," she added hastily.

Ben gave her hand a reassuring squeeze and she continued. "My mother got sick about then. She just kept getting weaker and weaker, and then she died." Her voice broke. "Instead of our grief drawing us closer, Papa and Paul and I seemed to get further and further from each other. Papa was gone more than ever with church work, and when he was home he seemed. . .angry all the time. As though his grief had made him even more impatient and harsh than he had been before."

She sighed. "Meanwhile, Paul spent more and more time with those fellows from school. I hardly saw him. But then one evening he came home earlier than usual. He disappeared into his room, and wouldn't come out. Finally, he let me in. He wouldn't say anything, just kept staring out his bedroom window." Raine closed her eyes in pain.

Though Raine kept her face averted from him, Ben could see the tears flowing down her cheeks. "Lucinda was found to be with child, and she accused Paul of being the father." She nearly choked on the words.

He stared at her face. Surely she didn't believe her brother was such a coward as to run away in the face of a lie like that, he thought. There must be something she wasn't telling him.

"Why did Paul have to leave home if he was falsely accused?"

"Papa didn't believe him. After Paul left, when her baby was born, Lucinda confessed who the real father was. But Papa didn't care. I begged him to search for Paul and tell him—but Papa didn't seem to even hear me." Her deep hurt and sense of betrayal were mirrored in her eyes as she looked up at him.

"Ah." He nodded, feeling helpless in the face of her pain. Apparently to her mind, their father's lack of trust was an adequate explanation for Paul running scared. Not knowing what else to do, he drew her into his embrace. "I'm so sorry," he whispered soothingly. He let her cry, knowing that the pain had been sharpened again by the retelling of the story. *Fortunately, she doesn't know the half of it,* he thought.

She pulled away from him, swiping at her eyes with her fingers. "When Lucinda accused Paul, the whole church turned against my brother. Papa told Paul that he had to apologize publicly to the church and marry Lucinda immediately, or he had to leave and never come back," she explained when she had composed herself.

"Paul pled with Papa to believe him, but Papa was adamant. He even forbid me to have any contact with Paul." Tears spilled down her cheeks. "When I tried to defend Paul, Papa became angry with me. He said I had to promise I would never mention Paul again—and if I refused, he wanted me to leave home." She shook her head. "I left. I couldn't bear to stay with Papa any more when he was so cold and angry. I went to work at the Mission and. . ." Her voice trailed away as she wiped away her tears with her hand.

"Before Paul left, he vowed one day to prove his innocence. He managed to send me a few messages in code, letting me know he was safe. Then I received one letter from him that was postmarked in Boston, but it had no return address. That was the last I heard from him, until you found me," she added sadly. Her shoulders slumped as she bowed her head.

Ben longed to draw her into his arms again. Instead, he place one finger under her chin and lifted her face to look into his own. "If Paul is alive, we'll find him," he promised, holding her gaze steadily.

"Thank you," she whispered.

ᴥ

Denver City, Colorado

Tom stomped out of the post office, clapping his Stetson on as he emerged into the bright sunlight.

"Shoulda stayed home," he muttered, untying Trixie.

All the way to Denver City he had hoped against hope that there would be a message waiting for him at the post office. A letter, a telegram, even a hastily scribbled postcard would have been a balm to his aching heart. But there was nothing.

You're a fool, he told himself. *What did you expect? Nobody even remembers that you exist,* his mind taunted him. If only he could write to her, maybe some of his loneliness would be eased, even if he never got an answer. But he didn't dare. . .

He kicked Trixie into a gallop, determined to escape the painful thoughts. Reining in abruptly at the edge of town, he paused. The open door of the Double Dare Saloon beckoned him into its dark, numbing comfort. He fought for just an instant against the magnetic force that drew him, then gave up in self-loathing.

Inside, he took a draught of blackstrap. Eyes watering, he set the tankard on the table with just the slightest twinge of guilt. What he wouldn't give to go back; to make a new start. . .

three

The arrival of the cargo ship the *Capernaum* was nothing exciting to the inhabitants of New York City, but it was one of the most thrilling experiences of Raine's life. As they sailed through the Narrows and into crowded New York Harbor, the sight of the famous "Lady of Liberty" brought tears to her eyes. She thought of Paul living in this welcoming land, and her hope of finding him alive and well was strengthened.

Passing the statue, the copper-clad towers and turreted brick of Ellis Island came into view on the left. Raine's heart went out to the swarms of immigrants crowding the decks of nearby ships. She had heard that sometimes the exhausted travelers had to wait as long as four days before a barge came to fetch them to the infamous island. It didn't seem fair that first- and second-class passengers were able to go right through customs, while their less fortunate brothers and sisters had to endure the endless examinations and inspections.

She turned her head as the *Capernaum* edged closely past a dilapidated sailing packet with the unlikely name of *Stella* gracing its bow. The mass of hopeful, fatigued faces tore at her heart. Where were all these people headed?

"Sad, isn't it?" Ben's quiet voice broke into her thoughts.

Raine nodded.

"Most of these ships are full of Polish and Russian Jews, fleeing from the pogroms."

Raine shook her head. Somehow, the suffering of other people always put one's own life into perspective. "We have a lot to be thankful for, don't we?"

Ben squeezed her hand. "That we do, Raine. That we do."

The *Capernaum* docked at Staten Island, awaiting the Ellis Island inspectors that would come aboard and conduct the medical examinations.

"How long does this usually take?" Raine asked.

"Well, it depends on how many passengers there are and how thorough the exams are." He smiled at her sparkling eyes and glowing skin. "I don't think you have much to worry about."

"I'm afraid Constance is worried."

Ben gazed into the ship's saloon where the larger woman sat waiting. "She does look rather nervous." Even the feathers on her Chanticleer hat were quivering. He shook his head, not understanding why a woman would wear a hat shaped like a rooster.

"I'll go sit with her," Raine suggested.

"That's a good idea. I need to run up to my quarters for the manifest, anyway. The inspectors always want to see it." He took another peek at Constance's hat as he walked away. The look on his face made Raine smother a giggle.

She went to the other woman and asked gently, "Are you ill, Constance?" The older woman looked wretched.

"No, dear. Not physically at least."

Raine raised her eyebrows.

"All those people on that ship." Constance gestured with her arm. "To think of my people enduring such terrible things that they had to flee their own country. . ."

"Perhaps God has sent you to America for a purpose, Constance."

Constance looked startled. "I guess I'd never thought of that, Raine. I was too busy feeling sorry for myself. . .but I've got it so much better than most, don't I?"

"I found a verse in Isaiah just before we began this voyage. It says, 'I will bring the blind by a way that they knew not; I will lead them in paths that they have not known: I will make darkness light before them, and crooked things straight. These things will I do unto them, and not forsake them.' I've gained much strength from that promise." She patted Constance's hand. "I know He'll guide you too if you ask Him."

Constance blew her nose, reminding Raine of an elephant she had once seen at the circus. "I feel so much better, dear.

You've helped me immeasurably."

Raine shook her head. "Not me, Constance. God."

The two women watched as the inspectors glanced at the ship's manifest. The uniformed men looked hassled, weariness etched on their brows. Handing the manifest back to Ben, they turned their attention to the medical reports.

Raine had easily passed the physical exam all passengers were required to take before they departed for America, but she still felt her heart beat a little faster as the men scrutinized the reports. She knew she didn't have anything to worry about; she had always been "healthy as a hog," as Papa would say.

"All right, line up over by the wall, please." The inspector's American accent sounded harsh, though his voice was pleasant.

Raine felt Constance stiffen as men made their way down the short line. The examination was mostly cursory for first-class passengers, since it was assumed none of them would be carrying disease.

She recalled Ben telling her of entire shiploads of people quarantined because of cholera, yellow fever, or typhoid. Victims of diphtheria or measles were often sent to the hospital on Ward's Island. She shivered. What a wretched welcome to America that would be.

"Open your mouth, please."

Raine obeyed and the man took a quick peek in her eyes as well, looking for the dreaded trachoma, she knew. He moved on to Constance. Raine watched the tail feathers on Constance's hat begin to dance. The poor woman looked like she would swoon any moment.

All went fine until the man heard the rattling in her chest. He raised his eyebrows. "Are you ill, Madam?"

Constance glared at him. "No."

He frowned. "Stay there. I'll be back in a minute."

Raine's heart sank as she watched him stride over to confer with the other inspector. "What's wrong, Constance?" she whispered.

"It's nothing, dear." Constance took a long breath, as though she were forcing herself to appear calm. "My chest tightens up and I get short of breath when I get nervous. Always goes away in a few minutes."

Raine knew what the man would say the instant he turned around.

"We'll have to take you to Ellis for a more thorough examination, Madam." He looked almost apologetic.

Raine closed her eyes, waiting to hear an explosion of tears. None came.

"Raine, will you come with me while I gather my things?" Constance's voice was calm.

Raine peered into the other woman's reddened eyes. Perhaps this was just the calm before the storm. Together they plodded down the stairs to Constance's cabin. Raine wracked her brain, trying to think of something to say.

"Well. I guess I will be going down some unfamiliar paths, just like that Scripture said, won't I?"

"I'm so sorry, Constance."

The older woman snorted. "Don't be. You know, as I was standing there waiting for them to make their decision, I started thinking on what you said about God sending me here for a purpose. All of a sudden I pictured all those poor people crowded on those boats headed for the Island." She cocked her head. "Maybe God wants me to be with my kin, so to speak."

Raine was speechless.

"They think I've got tuberculosis, you know."

Raine nodded.

"But I don't."

Raine nodded again, for lack of anything better to do.

"So. I'll just go to that Island and find out what God has for me. You know, I've been so miserable the past year, that I forgot all about Jesus. I guess He just needed to get my attention again. And He used you to help me get back on track."

Would wonders never cease. "I'm glad you feel that way about it," Raine finally managed. "You will write to me and let me know what happens?"

"You can bank on it, Reverend Thomas. That was quite a sermon you preached to me. You'll always hold a special place in my heart."

Reverend? She only had a second to ponder that one before she was nearly smothered in a giant bear hug. When she could breathe again, she was surprised to find her cheeks damp with tears.

The last she saw of her friend was a large bustle and an even larger smile disappearing into a swarm of haggard immigrants. "God go with you," Raine whispered.

As they disembarked from the ship, her heart lifted as she thought about her heavenly Father. His heart so loving that He even knew when a sparrow fell. Without a doubt, His eye was on Constance Rabinowicz.

❧

Raine was charmed by the thick accents and the hustle and bustle of the city, as Ben escorted her to the famous Buckingham Hotel on Fifth Avenue where she would stay the night, as her uncle had directed. Once inside, she gazed around in awe. The shining marble floor of the lobby reflected the multi-colored hues from the huge stained glass windows. Eight stories above her head, sunlight streamed through an enormous skylight. She had stepped into another world. Porters dashed in and out with baggage, lending a mood of excitement. Even the air seemed charged. She smiled. Maybe it was just being here, in America. It was, after all, the Land of Opportunity.

Her suite was beautiful. A fire crackled cheerily in the open fireplace, welcoming her into the bedchamber. She took a peek into the parlor, surprised to see another small room as well. A separate toilet room! Uncle John surely had spared no expense when he reserved this suite for her.

"I've got to get back to my crew, Raine," Ben said. "Shall we meet for supper at oh, six o'clock?"

"Six o'clock?" she moaned. "I think I'll starve by then!"

He chuckled. "I never knew a lady who had your appetite

before. I'll be back before you know it."

Once he was gone, she pushed back the red damask drapes to watch his retreating figure from the vantage of her fifth-floor window. He was even handsome from the back.

She continued to stand at the window long after he had disappeared, smiling, fascinated by the endless activity on the street below her.

Her smile froze as she noticed a man staring up at the hotel, his eyes fixed on her face. Something about him seemed familiar. . . Slipping behind the heavy drapery, she peered out again, but the man had disappeared from view.

Surely he was merely admiring the hotel, she thought. *Why would someone in New York be interested in me?* Feeling slightly uncomfortable, she turned to unpack her small bag. She was suddenly glad that she would be leaving for Boston in a couple of days.

ᷤ

Ben knocked on her door promptly at six o'clock.

Opening the door, Raine was taken aback as Ben presented her with a single yellow rose. "For you, milady," he said, bowing gallantly.

"Why, thank you, kind sir." Willing her heart to stop racing, she smiled up at him. "Shall we dine?"

"Indeed we shall." Ben escorted her to the hotel's dining room as if she were the queen of England. He seated her with a flourish. "Will you have the catfish or the pot roast? Or perhaps both? I know the sort of appetite you have."

She thumped him on the arm in mock indignation. In the end, she decided on the baked ham. It was cooked to perfection, but Raine found that despite her hunger, she was having a hard time keeping her attention on her supper. Ben's blue eyes were glowing with laughter, and his sun-lightened hair was set off by the dark suit he wore. She looked deep into his eyes as he smiled at her, suddenly eager to know everything about him. "Tell me about your childhood, Ben."

Instantly, the laughter slid from his eyes, replaced by an unreadable expression. "There's not much to tell, Raine," he said slowly.

"If you'd rather not. . ." she began, dismayed by his sudden change in mood.

"No," he said, pushing his pie around on his plate. "I want to tell you. I just. . .it's just hard to talk about, and I don't think you'll understand." Rising abruptly, he threw a tip on the table and offered Raine his arm. "Let's take a walk."

I must have ripped the bandage off of a festering wound, she realized as she glanced sideways at his expression. *At least he's willing to talk about it.* She breathed a quiet prayer for wisdom as they walked outside.

Ben led her to a small courtyard garden. Seating her on a bench, he paced back and forth in front of her. Finally sitting down, he ran his fingers through his hair, as though he were reluctant to begin his story.

"Ben." She placed a soothing hand on his cheek. "You can tell me."

Taking her hand, he held it tightly. "I'm an only child, and my parents were very strict with me. We went to church whenever the doors were open, and I was required to do quite a bit of Bible study and memorization, but. . ." He turned his face away from Raine, as though he didn't want her to see the pain etched there, but she could hear it in his voice as he continued. "There was no joy in our home. My parents were the most miserable people on earth, and they wanted me to be that way, too. They always quoted the Scripture 'to whom much is given, much is required.' " He shook his head. "The way they interpreted it was that if a person was happy, or well off financially, then that person must not really be in God's will, because if you're doing God's will, Satan will be attacking you all of the time."

No longer able to keep the bitterness from his voice, he turned to Raine. "I wasn't allowed to be happy, Raine. If I so much as laughed out loud, they accused me of being influenced by the devil and in need of discipline. They felt that if I wasn't being buffeted by Satan, then they needed to do the buffeting—and they used a willow switch to do it. I suppose they did it because they loved me. They were trying to push me into God's Kingdom after all."

Raine had never heard anything so sad in her life, nor such a mangling of Scripture. Even though her own father had been short-tempered and frequently absent, he had never twisted God's love into the harsh condemnation Ben's parents had apparently believed in.

"That's not the worst part of it, I'm afraid." Ben bowed his head. "I learned to put on an act, to pretend to be what my parents wanted me to be. When I grew older, my father made me go to seminary. I even graduated." Looking up at her, he let the tears fall unheeded. "But I'm a hypocrite, Raine. I feel nothing for God but bitterness and resentment—and yet I have a piece of paper that says I am a minister of the gospel." He turned away from her, struggling to control his weeping.

Raine pulled his head down, holding him as she would a hurting child.

"I left for Boston the day of graduation," he said in a hollow voice. "An acquaintance of my father's got me started in the shipping business. I worked my way up until eventually I owned my own line of ships. Whenever I get restless, I sail as the *Capernaum's* captain. I haven't seen my parents since the day I graduated from the seminary."

Pushing him away gently so she could see his face, Raine spoke with compassion. "Serving God doesn't have to be a drudgery, Ben. God is our Father. He loves us and wants us to have joy and peace."

"I know that in my mind, Raine, but I'm afraid," Ben whispered in despair. "I'm afraid that if I surrender to Him, He'll make me be like my father, or He'll ask me to do something that I just can't do."

"Total surrender is the only thing that will bring you the peace that you need, Ben," she stated quietly. "God will always give you the strength to do what He asks you to do."

He shook his head sadly. "I can't do it, Raine. I guess I'm a coward, but it just doesn't make sense to me." Seeing her stricken look, he put his hands on her shoulders. "I'm sorry. I shouldn't have burdened you with this."

She held his gaze steadily. "It will make sense to you one day, Ben Thackeray," she said, ignoring his apology. "One day, you will truly know peace."

༚

That night, she stayed on her knees for long hours before sleep finally claimed her. *I love him, Father,* she had cried, admitting out loud what her heart had known for weeks. *I want him to know You, to know Your peace. Please lead him to Christ, Father. Use me to minister Your love and joy to him. . . And please, Lord, bless Constance.*

Waking the next morning, her first thought was of a pair of sea-blue eyes and a warm smile. She stretched luxuriously, letting the newness of the day soak into her soul. Arising at last, she brushed out her dark hair until it shone. She reflected on the previous evening as she braided her hair into an intricate crown. *I hope Ben doesn't feel embarrassed over last night,* she thought, anxious to see him.

She dabbed on a bit of her favorite lilac perfume and adjusted the locket around her neck, then glanced in the mirror one last time. Glowing green eyes looked back at her, and she was sure Ben would be able to see her heart in her eyes. She smiled. It was wonderful to be in love, but she knew she must not run ahead of God's will for her. He was the one leading her along these new paths, and she reminded herself to wait on His direction.

She and Ben had decided to meet in the ladies' parlor, then go to the breakfast room together. Scanning the room eagerly, she was disappointed that Ben had not yet arrived. She sat down to wait, enjoying the way the morning sunshine filled the airy room. An ornate chandelier hung from the ceiling, and large ferns graced the perimeter of the room. Fresh flowers spilled down over pedestals, their bright fragrance permeating the air. The carpet as well as the walls were done tastefully in white, French gray, and gold. Here and there an early-rising guest sat reading a newspaper or leisurely working on some fancy needlework.

Raine's stomach growled loudly, and she frowned at the huge grandfather clock. It wasn't like Ben to be late. Shrugging, she decided a trip to the necessary room was in order. Maybe by the time she came out he would be there.

A small commotion near the door attracted her attention as she rose from her chair. She glanced in that direction, feeling something akin to panic wash over her as she caught a glimpse of the man walking in behind the porter. It was the man she had seen yesterday.

Nature's call forgotten, she made a beeline for the breakfast room. Daring a quick glance back, she was startled to see the blond-haired man sauntering toward her. His scarred face seared itself into her memory. Something about it seemed familiar. . .

"Good morning, Beautiful." She whirled.

"Ben!"

"What's wrong, Raine? Do I look that bad in the morning?" he teased.

She glanced over her shoulder. The man was nowhere to be seen. "You look just fine," she said weakly as relief flooded through her. "Let's eat breakfast."

The day went smoothly as they prepared for the trip to Boston. Except for the dark circles under Ben's eyes, no mention of the previous night was made. Having realized her love for him, however, Raine found it hard not to let it show. She knew in her heart that she could never marry a man who did not love her Lord, yet she was sure that God had brought Ben into her life for a special purpose.

❧

Two days later, Raine stood on the deck of the *Capernaum* once again, hardly able to quell the thrill of excitement running through her. She glanced up at Ben. "How long do you think it will take us to find Paul?"

An expression flickered across his face that made her uneasy, but he responded cheerfully enough, "Well, he left us a pretty good clue to follow."

Raine smiled as she thought of Uncle John and Aunt

Grace. It would be good to see them again. A sudden thought popped into her mind. "Where will you be staying, Ben?"

He frowned, staring over her shoulder into the distance. "I haven't decided yet."

His tone was so abrupt that Raine's heart sank. She turned back to gaze at the sea once again.

Surely he's not sorry that he promised to help me look for Paul, she thought. To her chagrin she felt tears begin to gather. *Maybe something came up and he doesn't know how to tell me. . .or maybe he just doesn't want to. . .*

"You don't have to help me find Paul," she muttered, staring blindly at the water. She felt his surprise as he pivoted to look at her.

Pulling her around to face him, he asked, "Why did you say that, Raine?"

"It just seems like you aren't very happy about it, so I thought maybe you were sorry that you had promised me you would help." Her voice was more petulant than she intended.

Ben winced. "I'm sorry it seemed that way, Raine. I really do want to help you find Paul. I just have a lot of things going on right now that need my attention."

Raine shrugged, feeling rather childish. "I shouldn't have even mentioned it."

Ben cupped her chin in his hand and smiled down at her. "We'll find him," he said finally. "Don't worry, Raine Ellen." Brushing her forehead with a soft kiss, he left to attend to his duties.

Raine had not missed the passion that had flared briefly in his eyes. She stood at the railing a while longer, daydreaming. What would it be like to be held in his strong arms, his lips meeting hers tenderly. . .

She wrinkled her brow as she remembered the cold look on his face earlier, but then she remembered again the tenderness in his voice when he said her name. Surely he cared for her. *Don't worry, Raine Ellen,* he had said.

Raine Ellen. She closed her eyes in sudden confusion. How

did Ben know her middle name? Paul had not been in the habit of calling her Raine Ellen.

The disfigured face of the man in New York popped into her mind. Shaking her head as if to clear out the suddenly disturbing thoughts, she sank down onto a nearby coil of rope. *Father,* she cried, *please show me Your way. I want to trust Ben, and I need to find Paul, but. . .*

. . .I will bring the blind by a way that they knew not; I will lead them in paths they they have not known. . . The Scripture from Isaiah echoed in her mind, and with it came peace. "Thank You, Lord," she breathed. Praying quietly, she poured out her thoughts and feelings to her ever-loving Father.

Opening her eyes at last, she was surprised to see Ben standing in front of her, a look of interest on his serious face.

"I'm not interrupting you, am I?" he asked hesitantly.

She shook her head.

"I just wanted to make you aware that a storm is coming."

She glanced quickly to the north, surprised to see a roiling mass of dark clouds. She hadn't even noticed when the sky had become overcast.

"I don't think it will be too bad, but you need to get off the deck. Are you afraid?" he asked, holding her shoulders lightly.

Looking up into his eyes, Raine pondered his question. *Yes, I'm afraid that I shouldn't love you so much,* her heart cried. "No, I'm not afraid of the storm," she answered out loud, watching in fascination as his eyes slowly darkened.

"Don't look at me that way, Raine," he growled. Pulling her into his arms, he drew her to him. Raine could feel his heart thudding as her head rested against the warmth of his chest. Releasing her abruptly, he caressed her face with his eyes. "Go to your cabin, Raine." His command was gentle. "I'll have Sully check on you later."

Mesmerized by his touch, she obediently turned to go. Reaching her cabin, she walked over to the small porthole. *Surely Ben wouldn't lie to me.* A hint of his aftershave lingered to tease her senses as she stared unseeingly at the turbulent waters. *My heart trusts him, but my mind is not so sure,* she mused. She flung herself down on her bunk and began to pray.

Raine awoke to a sharp knock on the door. Blinking in confusion as she saw sunlight streaming through the porthole, she padded to the door.

"Good morning, Sunshine!" Ben's blue eyes sparkled as they noticed her tousled hair. "I shouldn't have worried about you, Raine. You slept through the whole storm, didn't you?"

"I guess so." She was still groggy. Looking down self-consciously at her rumpled dress, she realized she must have fallen asleep while praying last night.

Ignoring her discomfort, Ben went on cheerily. "Well, everything went fine, and we'll be in Boston tomorrow, right on schedule. Do you feel like eating breakfast?"

Raine stared at him for a moment. "I need a few minutes to get ready," she said finally.

"Good. I'll meet you in my quarters in ten minutes." Swiftly kissing her on the lips, he was gone.

In his quarters? Touching her lips, Raine backed into her cabin. She groaned as she caught a glimpse of herself in the mirror. Several deep brown curls had worked themselves loose and were hanging down her back. Her cheeks were still rosy with sleep, and her dress was hopelessly wrinkled.

Sighing as she began to undo her hair, she pondered Ben's kiss. *We need to discuss some things before we go any further,* she decided. *There are just too many things that don't seem to fit together.*

Peering through the open door that led to his quarters twenty minutes later, she saw that he had cleared his desk. A steaming teapot and a tray of crumpets sat waiting where a mound of papers usually resided. "I thought just the two of us could have breakfast together this morning." He grinned at her in delight as her stomach growled loudly. "Do you think we have enough food?"

She moved into the room, leaving the door open behind her. "If you were a gentleman, you would have ignored that."

He laughed, and her heart ached. She wanted so much to believe in him; she hated to wipe the happiness from his face by questioning him. . . Halfway through breakfast, though, she decided to plunge in. "Ben, how did you find me?"

"My heart led me to you, darlin'," he teased, then laughed as she blushed. "Actually, I was wondering when you would get around to asking me that."

"I guess I've been so caught up with what you told me about Paul that I haven't given much thought to how you found me in the first place," she confessed, relieved that he seemed so open about it.

"Well," Ben began, leaning back in his chair. "Paul served on several of my ships at various times. He was a top-notch sailor, and a great conversationalist to boot."

Raine smiled at this, fondly remembering the long talks she and Paul had often had.

"After a while," Ben continued, "Paul and I began to develop a real friendship. He often came to my quarters, and we would talk late into the night. You were one of his favorite topics of conversation," he added, smiling at her.

She wrinkled her nose, asking the question that had been bothering her for some time. "Then how could you have possibly missed the fact that we were brother and sister?"

For a long moment, Ben studied the bite of cheese he held on his fork. "I've asked myself the same question, Raine," he said at last. He shifted his gaze back to hers. "I have finally come to the conclusion that Paul purposely misled me."

"What?" Raine was incredulous. "Why would he do that?"

"I don't know. The only thing I could come up with was that maybe he was trying to protect you."

"Protect me from what?"

His index finger traced the wet ring his tea cup had made on the desktop. "I don't know," he admitted. "He told me his name was Paul Oliver."

"He didn't use his own name?" She shook her head slowly. "I suppose if he would have gone by Paul Thomas, you would have known right away that we were related. I guess I really don't know much about the person Paul was after he left home," she concluded sadly. "But I still can't figure out why he never wrote me any more letters after that one from Boston. The last letter I received from Paul was postmarked June 6, 1900."

"1900! I didn't even meet Paul until 1901, then the *Aramathea* sank in 1903." Ben was astonished. "I looked for you for three years, so that means you haven't heard from Paul in. . .six years?"

Raine nodded. "That's why I was so shocked when you gave me the locket. I had given up hope. But how did you find me?" she asked, anxious to hear the rest of the story.

"I first met Paul on the *Galilee*. He was new to the crew, and I keep a pretty sharp watch on the men. I don't question them about their past, but I expect them to do an honest day's work for me." Ben explained. "Paul never talked much about his past, except you, and I didn't pry. Once in a while he would mention something that made me wonder what had happened, but I never asked."

He shook his head before continuing. "One day after we had become quite close friends, Paul showed me the locket. He didn't give it to me then, but told me that it contained a message for you. He made me promise that I would find you and give it to you if something ever happened to him."

"When was that?"

"It was before we set sail on the *Aramathea*. I don't know what prompted him to ask me at that time," Ben added thoughtfully.

Am being pursued. The phrase from the message in the locket flitted through her mind. "Could Paul have been running from someone, and he was afraid that the person would harm me as well?" she wondered out loud. "Maybe that's what he meant by 'am being pursued'."

"I just don't know."

"Anyway, how in the world did Paul expect you to find me?"

Ben smiled at her over his glass. "He showed me your photograph, for one thing. I used to look at it every night while Paul and I were talking. After a while, I was pretty familiar with your features."

Raine looked down in embarrassment. She knew what photograph Ben was referring to. She had had it taken when she was eighteen, and had given it to Paul on his birthday.

That's how Ben knew my middle name, she realized with swift insight, remembering what she had written on the back of the large photograph. "To my one and only—Love, Raine Ellen." Raine had meant her one and only brother, but she could see how the inscription might be taken wrong.

She glanced up at Ben when he chuckled softly. "I memorized every line of your lovely face, Raine."

She involuntarily covered the birthmark on her temple, feeling her cheeks grow hot. This man had a way of making her feel things she wasn't accustomed to feeling.

"Other than the image of your face stamped on my memory, I didn't have much to go on. Paul had given me the address of your home in St. Albans, of course—but when I went there, your father told me you were gone and refused to tell me anything more. He practically slammed the door in my face."

Raine shook her head. *Oh Papa, what a mess you've made.*

Ben took her hand. "I guess it was fate that I found you, then," he said lightly. "After I reached the dead end in St. Albans, I didn't know where else to look. I had pretty much given up hope of ever finding you—and then after all these years, I saw you on the wharf. Something about your face compelled me to look closer, and well, you know the rest."

Raine felt a thrill of excitement go through her as Ben explained how he had found her. "I don't believe in fate, Ben," she stated with conviction. "I believe that God allowed you to find me when the time was right."

He looked thoughtful. "That may be, Raine," he said slowly, gently pressing her hand to his lips.

❧

El Paso County, Colorado

The rain pounded relentlessly, turning the thirsty prairie land of the Crooked P Ranch into one huge mud puddle. Unseasonable rains had begun two weeks earlier. The constant dripping showed no signs of letting up as Tom paced back and forth in frustration.

Finally dropping into his chair in disgust, he absently rubbed his fingertips over the still-sensitive scar on his cheek. *I'm going to go crazy if I can't get out of here soon,* he told himself. After keeping himself busy with all of the things he could think of to do inside, there was nothing left to do but wait for the rain to subside. *This must be how Noah felt,* he thought without humor.

The idea crossed his mind to go to the bunkhouse, but he decided he was in no mood for the never-ending jokes and loud disagreements that he was sure to find there. His eyes wandered to the bookcase. He sighed. "I've read every single one of those books at least twice," he complained to the empty room, knowing from experience that if he didn't find something to occupy his mind, his thoughts would become too painful. Heaving himself out of his chair, he walked to the window once again, swearing softly as the rain picked up its intensity.

As he turned away sharply, his eye fell on the large Bible lying on the bookshelf. Deliberately, he went to the kitchen and poured himself a fresh cup of coffee, then returned once again to the warm living room. Drawn like a magnet to the Book that he had not opened in years, he took it down with reluctance, blowing the dust off the worn leather cover. He hated himself for trembling, but he could not help it as he turned to the inscription he knew was written on the first page. Though he knew it by heart, Tom read it again through eyes blurred with tears. Closing the Bible, he laid his head down and wept. *I don't know how to come back to You after all this time,* he cried in his heart. *God, help me. . .*

He raised his head, glancing down as he felt the heavy weight of the Bible in his lap. He must have fallen asleep. Rising, he placed the Bible back on the shelf. The rain pattered a gentle lullaby as he blew out the lamp.

four

Raine woke with a start. Today the *Capernaum* would arrive in Boston! Rolling over, she reflected on what she had learned the day before. There were still so many unanswered questions. Why had she suddenly stopped hearing from Paul so long ago if he were alive and well? Why had he used an assumed name?

She had known right away why Paul had chosen to go by Paul Oliver; their mother's father, their beloved grandfather, had been named Oliver Cox. That much made sense to her. *But what did he want me to find in Boston? And what did the water erase?* She fingered the locket that hung around her neck, recalling one of their last conversations.

"I'll prove that I'm innocent, Raine," Paul vowed before he left. "Papa may have disowned me, but one day he'll have to eat his words. Then I'll never come back, even if he begs me to."

Raine was shocked at the bitterness in her brother's voice. "Paul—"

"Come with me, Ray," he pled.

She wavered, but in the end decided she had to stay. "Where would we go?" she asked, tears flowing down her face. "How would we support ourselves?" She shook her head. "No, you'll be better off on your own for now. But I'll find you after a little while, and then we'll be together again."

She hadn't known then she too would be leaving her father so soon, making her own way in the world. That had been so many years ago. "I'm finally coming, Paul," she whispered.

The *Capernaum* slipped silently into the harbor like a turtle sliding off a rock. Unable to stop herself, Raine scanned the crowded wharf. *Stop it, Raine,* she chided herself. *Paul doesn't even know that you're on this ship, much less in Boston.* She tried to ignore the thought that her brother might not even be alive. God had brought her here for a reason.

ॐ

"Good morning, Sunshine!" Ben greeted her as she walked through the door of his quarters. He always felt like his day had begun when she walked through the door. "Are you ready for the big search to begin?"

"More than ready!"

"I'll be done in a minute." He indicated some papers on his desk. "Then I'll be free to escort you to your uncle's house."

Raine smiled her thanks. Choosing a large leather chair, she sat down and closed her eyes. Ben could tell she was trying to quell her excitement and nervousness. He stood up and picked up her bags. "Are you ready to go?"

She was on her feet in an instant. "Lead on, kind sir!"

They bounced and jounced over the stone-paved streets for what seemed hours before Ben stopped the carriage in front of a large brick house on Joy Street. He heard Raine gave a sigh of relief as she craned her neck to view the old house.

"It's beautiful," she breathed, taking in the well-cared-for lawns and sparkling flower beds. Ben saw a look of peace settle over her face as she turned to him. "Would you please come in and meet my family?" she asked. "I know they would like to meet you."

Ben squeezed her hand. "I would love to."

The huge front door flew open. "Raine!" A tall, slim woman rushed to the carriage.

"Aunt Grace!" Raine was out of the carriage and in her aunt's arms in a flash.

Pushing Raine away after a moment, Grace looked her niece up and down. "You're the picture of your mother," she cried, pulling Raine into her embrace once again.

"Ahem." Ben looked beyond Raine's aunt to see her uncle beaming at her. "Is it my turn yet?" he asked in a gravelly voice.

"Oh, Uncle John! It's so good to see you!"

Finally released from her uncle's bear hug, Raine seemed

to remember Ben, standing silently next to the carriage. Walking over to him, she shyly took his hand.

"Uncle John, Aunt Grace, this is Ben Thackeray." Raine's cheeks grew rosy at her family's knowing looks.

Her aunt and uncle welcomed Ben cordially. "Come into the house, both of you. We have cool lemonade waiting."

"I'm afraid I need to get back to my ship, but thank you anyway," Ben apologized. "Raine, may I speak with you a moment?"

Raine's aunt and uncle graciously excused themselves, leaving Ben and Raine alone. "I need to stay on the ship tonight, Raine. The crew is waiting for some last-minute instructions from me before I turn the ship over to the first mate and they take their leave. I'll be back to see you at the end of the week. That should give you some time to get settled in and. . ."

"But I'll miss you!" she blurted. She lowered her eyes in embarrassment, and he knew she missed the tenderness he couldn't hide at her impulsive words.

Lifting her chin, he saw a hint of tears shimmering in her dusky green eyes. "I'll miss you, too, love," he murmured, pulling her into his embrace. Feeling her soft lips tremble beneath his, he kissed her deeply, the scent of her warm skin making his blood pound. He put her from him then, breathing hard. "I don't know what you're doing to me," he whispered huskily.

She gazed up at him, her heart in her eyes.

"Don't look at me like that, Raine," he groaned, longing to crush her to him again.

She touched her fingertips to his lips. "I'll see you soon, Ben," she whispered.

He waved from the carriage, the light scent of lilacs still clinging to his senses. *If you had any sense, you'd marry that woman right now.*

❧

Raine waved as Ben's carriage rolled away from her. *You are entirely too attached to that man,* she scolded herself as she watched him turn the horses. She stood rooted to the spot until he was out of sight. Entering into the dim coolness of the foyer, she braced herself for the barrage of questions that was sure to come.

"Raine! Who is Ben? Is he a captain of a ship? When did you. . ."

"Whoa, Grace." Uncle John chuckled. "Let's let the little gal get settled before we interrogate her."

Raine smiled at her uncle gratefully, enjoying his Americanized accent. "We'll have a heart to heart talk later, Auntie Grace. I promise."

"I'm sorry, dear," her aunt apologized. "It's just that we're so glad to see you, and your Ben is so handsome, and. . ."

Uncle John winked at Raine. "Why don't you go and see about that lemonade while I help Raine with her things?" Giving his wife no time to reply, he started up the stairs. "Coming, Raine?"

Raine nodded. "We'll be down in a minute, Auntie," she called to her aunt who had already disappeared down the hallway.

♈

"So. Start at the beginning, Raine." They were all seated at the enormous oak table with tall glasses of lemonade.

"It's a long story," Raine warned them.

"We have plenty of time," Grace assured her. "Besides, we haven't seen you in years."

"Well, let's see," Raine began. "You two moved to America in. . ."

"1886."

"So that was while Mama was still living and. . ."

"We're so sorry we couldn't come for her funeral, Raine," Grace interrupted again. "I felt so bad being so far away at a time like that."

"I'm sure you would have been there if you could," Raine said soothingly. "We surely felt your prayers."

"How's that scalawag brother of yours?" Uncle John asked, as though he were trying to change the subject tactfully. "We haven't heard much news about him lately. 'Course we haven't heard much news at all."

Raine stared at them. Was it possible they didn't know about Paul? "Papa didn't tell you about him?" she asked cautiously.

"No." Grace looked puzzled. "The last we heard, he was sailing, and we assumed that he was happy and well. Oh dear, did something happen to him?"

Raine stared at her aunt. *Something is wrong here. . .*"How did you know Paul was a sailor?" she asked in a strained voice.

"Why, your papa told us in one of his letters a few years back. Raine, are you ill, dear?"

Raine was trembling. *How could Papa have known where Paul was? Could he have known all this time? Why didn't you tell me, Papa? Oh Paul. . .* A wave of darkness rushed over her.

"She's so pale, John." Raine heard her aunt's hushed voice.

"Shh, she's coming to."

Raine sat up, feeling like a hive full of bees was buzzing in her head. Realizing she was no longer at the table, she looked questioningly at John.

"You fainted, honey. I carried you to the sofa."

How embarrassing. She had never fainted before in her life. Suddenly recalling the conversation that had prompted her shock, she buried her face in her hands.

Aunt Grace enfolded her in a firm embrace. "It's going to be all right, Raine. Go ahead and cry."

A dam broke inside of Raine at her aunt's motherly touch. Silent weeping gave way to great heaving sobs. It had been so long since she had felt another woman's comforting touch.

Finally collecting herself, she looked up at her aunt. "Thank you," she whispered.

"Do you feel like talking about it, dear, or do you just want to rest now?" Grace's concern was evident on her face.

"I'm fine now." Raine gave her a watery smile. "It was just such a shock."

"I'm afraid we don't understand what's going on here,

Raine," her uncle said.

"I don't know if I understand either, Uncle John," Raine said wryly. "But I'll explain what I know."

She started at the beginning, describing the circumstances that led to Paul leaving home. Tears of anger stood in Grace's eyes as her niece recounted the story.

"I'd like to take that brother of mine over my knee," Raine heard her mutter at one point.

"After that," Raine concluded her story, "I received one letter from him that was postmarked in Boston, but that was all until Ben brought me the locket."

Grace sat up abruptly as Raine ended her story. "Boston!" She looked at her husband. "Remember that time I thought I saw him outside that—" She broke off and her forehead puckered.

"You thought you saw Paul?" Raine asked eagerly. "When?"

Grace shook her head. "It was some years ago. I was looking out the window of the carriage, on my way to the dressmaker's, and I saw a man come out of a tavern. He was. . . well, from the way he walked, he was obviously under the influence. But when I first looked at him, I thought I recognized him. He looked just like Paul—but it was so quick. I told the driver to stop and go back, but the man, whoever he was, had disappeared. When I got home, your uncle told me I must have been imagining things, and I put it out of my mind." She shook her head again. "So he did come here, just like your father told us. Why wouldn't he have come to see us at least once?"

"Father said. . .? You knew. . .?" Raine's head whirled with confusion. Suddenly it was all too much for her. "I think I need to get some rest," she said apologetically. "Maybe a good night's sleep will help me sort all of this out."

"I think that's a good idea, dear." Grace patted Raine's cheek softly. "We can talk more tomorrow. Why don't you just head upstairs, and I'll. . ."

"Wait, Grace." John put a large hand on each woman's shoulder. "I think we should pray before Raine goes upstairs."

Raine nodded gratefully. "I would like that very much, Uncle John." She dashed away a tear, and joined hands with her aunt and uncle.

"Dear Father," John began, "thank You for bringing Raine here safely. You are so good to us, Lord. Now I ask that You give us peace concerning Paul. Let Raine especially feel Your peace this evening, and allow her to have a restful night's sleep. Please minister to Paul wherever he is. Keep him safe, and draw him continually to You. . ."

Raine felt a sense of peace wash over her as she listened to her uncle's heartfelt prayer. "Yes, Father," she whispered.

"And touch the young man Ben wherever he is tonight," her uncle continued. "Let him feel Your love in a way he's never felt it before. Thank You for hearing us, Father. In Jesus' name, amen." John cleared his throat. "Now, off to bed with you, young lady!"

"Thank you, Uncle John." Halfway up the stairs, Raine couldn't resist turning around. "Why did you pray for Ben?" she asked curiously.

Uncle John winked. "Good night, Raine."

Raine didn't think she'd be able to rest at all, but sleep overtook her quickly, the words of her uncle's prayer ringing in her ears.

⁂

"Rise and shine!" Raine's eyes flew open. The sun was streaming in through the window, and Aunt Grace was knocking on her door.

"Come in, Auntie," she called.

Grace perched on the side of Raine's bed. "How did you sleep, dear?"

"Very soundly." Raine grinned.

"Good!" Grace was pleased. "Come down and have breakfast with us before your uncle leaves for the office." Grace paused at the door. "After all, there's still some things we need to talk about," she said in mock sternness, giving Raine a pointed look.

"I know, I know. I'll tell you all about Ben. Now let me get ready for breakfast!" Raine shooed her aunt out the door. She was anxious to learn what her father had told her aunt and uncle, but the thought of Ben made her smile. She pictured his blue eyes and golden hair as she hurriedly dressed. The thought of his good-bye kiss yesterday did funny things to her insides. How could she miss him so much already?

"Well now, here's the world traveler!" Raine's uncle greeted her cheerily. "How did you like sailing, anyway? I didn't get a chance to ask you yesterday."

Raine considered the question. "Well, I wouldn't want to be at sea all the time, but I did enjoy the voyage for the most part."

"Especially with such a handsome man for a captain!" Grace noted.

"Grace!"

"It's all right, Uncle John. Auntie is dying to hear about Ben, so I'd better oblige her or we'll never hear the end of it."

John rolled his eyes good-naturedly. "I suppose."

Grace settled into a chair, pouring herself a cup of tea. "I'm ready." Raine related the story of how she'd met Ben and all that had happened since then, enjoying her aunt's eager expression.

"And?" Grace prompted when Raine stopped talking.

"And what?" Raine hedged, knowing what question was coming next.

"Do you love him?"

"Grace!" Uncle John scolded again.

Raine blushed and dropped her eyes, but not before her aunt saw the answer to her question.

"I knew it!" Grace said excitedly. "Does he love you, child?"

"I think so, Auntie." Raine answered truthfully. "We've never talked about it, but. . ."

"Does Captain Ben love our Lord?" Uncle John asked seriously.

Raine's face was troubled. "Not yet, Uncle John. But he wants to." Raine explained Ben's past to them, her eyes softening as she remembered the yearning that had been in Ben's voice.

"Well, wanting to know God is the best place to start," John said thoughtfully. "I'll be praying for him."

Raine smiled her gratitude at the two dear people across the table from her. "I love you two," she said quietly. "And now I need to know what my father told you."

"Show Ray the letters from Richard," Uncle John said to his wife. "Maybe they will help clear up some of the questions." He got up and gave Raine a peck on the cheek. "You're a special gal." Kissing his wife as well, he headed for the door.

Raine looked at her aunt eagerly. "Did you save all my father's letters?"

"I think so." Her aunt was digging in the desk drawer. "Yes, here they are." Raine grasped the packet of letters from her father, her heart thudding at the possibility of what they might hold.

"Here, let me help you with the dishes, Aunt Grace," she offered, reluctantly laying the letters down as she realized her aunt was clearing the table.

"No, no, I'm fine. You just go on ahead upstairs. Take your time." Grace fairly pushed her niece from the kitchen.

Raine sat at the desk in her room, her hands trembling. Breathing a quick prayer for strength, she slowly opened the first letter.

Dear Grace and John,
Hope this letter finds you both well. We are all fine here. Paul and Raine are doing well in school, and Ellen is. . .

Glancing at the date, Raine realized that this letter had been written long before Paul had left home. Laying it aside, she sorted the rest of the letters by date, then started reading with the ones dated the year Paul left.

The first letter she read contained nothing but chatty, newsy information about the church, the weather, and so on. The next was the same, and Raine laid it aside with a sense of disappointment. Scanning the third letter quickly, her brother's name caught her eye. Tucked in among some pleasantries, her father had written casually, *Paul has left home to find work. He'll be gone for some time.* Left home to find work! Raine was appalled at her father's twisting of the truth. She hastily read the rest of the letter, but found no more reference to Paul. She put it down in growing anger.

The next three letters gave just passing mention of Paul, saying only that he would still be away for a while. Raine opened the next letter with a sigh of frustration, suddenly a sentence leapt out at her.

> *Paul is living in Boston when he's not at sea. Perhaps he will come and visit you, but I hear he's pretty busy.*

Raine clenched her teeth. How could he? How could Papa have known where Paul was and not told her? She looked at the date at the top of the letter. She was still living at home, she realized.

Scanning two or three more letters, she felt nauseated at the trivial manner her father spoke of her beloved brother. *Paul is enjoying the life of a sailor* and *Paul is thriving in Boston.* And meanwhile Raine hadn't even known for certain if Paul was still alive.

Abruptly, a thought struck her. What if Papa had made all of this up? What if he really didn't know what Paul was doing all that time, but he wanted to make it sound like he did?

Hurriedly opening another letter, Raine froze as she read the first line.

> *Thank God, Paul survived the sinking of his ship, the* Aramathea.

Raine read the words again, letting their meaning soak into her shocked brain. Her brother was alive! Putting her head down on the desk, she wept with thankfulness. Rejoicing at the news that she had waited so long to hear, it took her a few moments to react to the fact that her father must have known where Paul was all along. Her anger began to build. *If Papa knew that Paul had survived the sinking of the* Aramathea, *then he must know where he is now,* she reasoned.

Why didn't you tell me, Papa? Why did you let me wonder in agony all this time, not knowing if my brother was dead or alive? Then a new thought jolted her. *If Paul is alive, why hasn't he contacted me? If he wrote to Papa, why wouldn't he want me to know about it?* She shook her head as if to clear out the questions. Surely Paul would want her to know where he was, wouldn't he?

She stood up and stretched. *I can't make any sense of all this.* She skimmed the rest of the letters, surprised to see that there were no more references to Paul, except in the last letter which said only, *Haven't heard from Paul in a while.*

She gathered the letters into a neat stack. *I guess I'll just have to wait until Ben can help me follow the directions in the locket,* she decided. It seemed forever since she had said good-bye to him in front of Uncle John's house.

☙

"How would you like to see some of the sights of our fair city tomorrow, Raine?" John smiled at his niece later that day.

Raine nodded with enthusiasm, her mouth full of banana bread. She would be fat and lazy if she stayed at Aunt Grace's much longer.

"First we'll go see Paul Revere's grave at the Old Granary Burial Ground. Then perhaps a drive down by the Charles River would be in order. After that we'll stop for tea at. . ."

"We don't want to wear her out the first week she's here, John."

"Don't worry about me, Auntie. I'm used to being busy."

Though she would not have admitted it, by the next afternoon Raine was more than happy to stop for tea. In one morning's time, she had learned more American history than in all her years of schooling. Her favorite place by far had been the Park Street Church where Uncle John regaled them with an account of the church's colorful past.

"They call this 'Brimstone Corner,' " he had said, indicating the site. "I guess that's because of all the fiery sermons preached here over the years." He chuckled. "Actually, I think it's because brimstone used for making gunpowder was stored in the church's basement during the War of 1812."

"And this church was the place where 'America the Beautiful' was first sung in public." Grace added proudly.

John nodded. "That's true. It's also the only church I know of that had a fountain in the pastor's study."

"What?" Raine lifted her eyebrows. This she had to hear.

"Yes, ma'am. A few years ago, I think it was 1895 or so, a workman in the Tremont Street Subway accidentally stuck his pick into a huge water main. A geyser spurted upwards so forcefully that it broke the windows out of the pastor's study. The whole room was filled with mud."

"You're teasing me, Uncle John."

"No, I'm not! We were there for the evening service." He chuckled. "The reverend was not amused. He called the subway 'an infernal hole' and 'an unchristian outrage.' " Uncle John was clearly tickled.

"That poor man." Aunt Grace sighed. "We haven't seen him in years. I hope he has been able to overcome the shock."

Raine giggled.

They savored their tea, enjoying each other's company. Soon the afternoon found them strolling along on Pinckney Street. Almost ready to call it a day, the threesome had decided to stop and admire the lovely homes that lined the famous street.

"Look at this little tunnel!" Raine called to Grace. Peering through the wrought iron gate, she saw that the narrow passageway led under the house to a beautiful courtyard garden. Standing on tiptoe to see better, she felt the gate catch on her voluminous skirts. Still standing on tiptoe, she tried to extricate herself. She was afraid if she moved too much, the thin fabric would tear. And her favorite blue silk, too, she thought mournfully.

She glanced in her aunt's direction, but she and Uncle John were energetically discussing the architecture of the house. Besides, Uncle John would tease her unmercifully if he had to rescue her from a gate. *This is ridiculous,* she scolded herself. *I can't just stand here stuck on this gate forever. Besides, what if the owner wants to visit his garden? Excuse me, miss. Could I just swing you aside to get through my gate please?* She rolled her eyes.

"Raine!"

Prepared to yank her skirt loose, her hand froze. Had someone whispered her name?

"Raine Thomas!"

Her heart hammering, she surveyed the grounds. There, in the bushes. "Who are you?" she called.

The blond man stepped away from the shrubbery, his disfigured face in plain view. "Raine, I've been wanting—"

She heard the tear of fabric as she fled.

❧

After that a cloud of anxiety seemed to descend over Raine. Her anxiousness increased as the week wore on and she did not see Ben. Finally on Friday afternoon, a note was delivered to the house.

> *Dear Raine,*
> *I'm finally free of my duties. May I come by tonight?*
> *Send a reply back with the messenger.*
>
> > *Yours,*
> > *Ben*

Joyously, she scribbled a response. Handing the note back to the young messenger, she danced into the kitchen. "Auntie, Ben is coming tonight!"

Grace took in the sparkling eyes and glowing face of the younger woman. "I'd better bake an extra pie, then," she said with a twinkle in her eye. "You'd best get upstairs and get ready."

"Thank you, Aunt Grace." Raine pecked her aunt's heat-flushed cheek. "What do you think I should wear?"

Her aunt rolled her eyes. "Good heavens, Raine. You act like you haven't seen the man in a year! You look beautiful in anything. Now get out of my kitchen!" she ordered with a smile.

Raine dutifully trotted up the stairs, only to return minutes later. "How does my hair look like this?"

Grace glanced up from her pie crust. "You look lovely, dear. I'm sure your Ben will be pleased. Now, if I'm to get these pies done. . ."

"I'm going, I'm going!" Raine backed out of her aunt's kitchen, almost knocking her uncle over. "Uncle John! I'm sorry. I didn't know you were standing there!"

"Apparently not," he agreed wryly. "You look especially glowing tonight. Are we going to be graced with the company of the dashing Captain Ben?" he teased.

Raine's cheeks grew hot. Were her feelings that transparent?

"He'll be here at six."

"Good, good!" Uncle John boomed. "I'd like to spend some time getting to know the man that stole my gal's heart." Noting the look of consternation on her face, he patted her hand. "Don't worry, honey. I won't embarrass you."

Raine gave him a weak smile. This evening might not go exactly as she had anticipated it. . .

The knock at the door at five minutes before six sent butterflies racing through Raine's stomach. *Stop being silly,* she scolded herself in vain. Opening the door, her heart leapt at the sight of Ben's tall form.

He touched her cheek with a gentle hand. "Hello, Raine," he said softly.

She couldn't take her eyes off of his face as he stepped through the door. "It seems like it's been so long since I've seen you. . . I'm so glad you could come," she whispered.

"So am—"

"Well, well!" Uncle John's voice preceded him into the foyer. "Gracie, come greet our guest!"

The spell was broken. Raine giggled as she shrugged at

Ben, watching him shift gears mentally.

"It's nice to see you again, Captain Ben!" Uncle John pumped Ben's hand with enthusiasm.

Though obviously taken aback at the zestful welcome, Ben gave Raine's uncle a broad smile. "Thank you for having me, sir."

"Now, none of that, young man. You must call us Grace and John." Grace's manner put Ben at ease instantly. "We're not very formal at this house," she added.

Soon the men were settled in the parlor to await supper. Raine disappeared into the kitchen with Grace, but couldn't resist peeking in at Ben. Uncle John had launched into one of his favorite stories, delighted to tell it to someone who had never heard it before.

"I don't think those two will lack for things to talk about," she said.

Grace smiled. "Your uncle would gab all night if I let him."

By the time they sat down to the huge meal Grace had prepared, Ben felt like he had known Raine's aunt and uncle all his life. Bowing his head as John said the blessing, he was unprepared for the emotions that assailed him. The biscuits had cooled before John finished praying, but Ben hardly noticed the length as he felt the joy and thankfulness emanating from the older man's words.

What would it have been like to grow up in a family like this? Visions of his long-faced father droning out a mournful prayer filled his thoughts. Shaken more than he cared to admit, he was quiet for a few minutes before entering into the light banter going on around the table. Soon he was regaling them with stories of his own.

As the supper was nearly over Ben began yet another story, this one about his partner's aunt, who had a habit of sneaking around Ben's office making sure that Ben was "conducting business in the proper manner."

"Yes, that Vida Daniels is one lady to reckon with," Ben said, leaning back comfortably in his chair.

"Daniels!" Raine's eyes flew wide with surprise. "But I thought she was—"

Ben grinned. "You thought she was what?"

"Younger," she said lamely. She dropped her eyes in embarrassment, obviously recalling the two elderly women who had been in Ben's office that morning, and then she giggled in spite of herself. Fascinated, he watched the flicker of expressions cross her face.

Grace gave John a pointed look and the two excused themselves. "I'm sure we'll be seeing you again, Ben," Grace said. "You're always welcome."

Ben thanked his hosts, then turned to Raine as they left the room.

She said softly, searching his face, "I've missed you this week."

"I missed you, too. It didn't seem the same on the *Capernaum* without you to brighten my day."

"I've been waiting for you to come so I could tell you my good news." Her eyes had taken on a glow. "You'll never guess."

He raised his eyebrows. "Does it have anything to do with a missing brother?"

"He's not missing anymore! At least, I don't think he is." Her brow clouded suddenly.

"I'm afraid I lost you there, Raine."

"Well, it seems that Papa knew where Paul was all along."

"Was?"

She frowned. "That's the problem. From what I gather, Paul survived the shipwreck, but Papa hasn't heard from him since."

An enormous wave of relief washed over him at her words. Taking her hand, he held it tightly. "Raine, you don't know how glad I am to hear that Paul is alive. You see," his voice broke, "as the captain of the *Aramathea* when it sank, all this time I've felt guilty for killing your brother, but now. . ." He swallowed the lump in his throat.

Raine stroked his hand with a gentle touch. "It wasn't your

fault, Ben," she said quietly. "Even if Paul had died, it wouldn't have been your fault. I'm sure you did the best job you could." Her words felt like soothing balm on a burning wound. "We all make mistakes, Ben," she said. Her sincerity was reflected in her eyes. "But what matters now is that Paul is alive—and we need to find him!"

Ben reached out and caught her chin in his hand, staring deep into her eyes. When he fell in love with her picture so long ago, he didn't realize that her lovely face was only a cover for her inner beauty.

She colored at his gentle touch but didn't look away. Tenderly lowering his mouth to hers, he felt her sigh. He pulled her tight against his chest, his heart pounding.

Stop now, he told himself. Pushing her gently away, he sank down into the kitchen chair. He didn't dare look at her, or he would take her in his arms again. "Go put on the tea kettle or something, would you, woman?"

Raine smiled at his gruff tone. She knew as well as he did that neither one of them had wanted the moment to end.

Hours later, they sat in the deepening twilight, the porch swing creaking underneath them. "Let's read the message in the locket again now that we're finally in Boston," Ben suggested. "Tomorrow we can go find that address."

She reached for the locket she always kept around her neck, then paused. "There's something else I need to talk to you about."

His throat tightened at her serious tone. "Am I in trouble?"

"No, but I may be." Taking a deep breath, she told him about the man she had seen in New York and now again in Boston.

❧

"Well, here we are!" Ben said the next morning as he drew the carriage to a halt in front of a large, two-story house on High Street.

Raine studied the old house as if it would speak and tell her where Paul was. Could it be possible that he lived here? She eyed the lacy curtains and well-tended herb garden dubiously.

"Are you ready to go in, Raine?" Ben asked.

She sighed. "I guess so. I just don't know what to expect. What if I find out something I don't want to know?"

Ben squeezed her hand as he helped her out of the carriage. 'We'll cross that bridge when we come to it. I'll be right with you the whole time."

She tried to give him a brave smile as they walked up to the house, but she knew he must feel her trembling as they climbed up the wooden porch steps. *The Lord is my shepherd,* she told herself. *I shall not want.*

"Do come in!" a bright voice called in response to Ben's knock.

Raine stared at Ben, frozen. He gave her a gentle push through the door.

"Who is it, please?" the voice asked.

Raine cautiously made her way into the cheery living room, stopping short as she saw an elderly woman in a wheelchair. Her snowy hair was caught up in an attractive bun, and a lacy shawl was draped over her thin shoulders. A smile lit her still beautiful face as she held out her hands in welcome. "Come in, dear," she said kindly, her British accent warming her words. "How can I help you young people?"

Raine didn't know what she had expected to find, but this certainly wasn't it. Perhaps this wasn't the right address.

"I'm Raine Thomas," she said uncertainly.

"Oh!" The woman's wrinkled face lit up at once, her bright eyes sweeping up to Raine's right temple. "I knew you would come!"

Automatically, Raine put a protective hand over the birthmark. Why was this woman staring at her so intently?

Oblivious to Raine's bewildered expression, the woman examined her, then sat back with a satisfied expression on her face. "You're even more beautiful than Paul said you were." She beamed at Raine. "And who might this be?" she asked, smiling at Ben.

"I'm Ben Thackeray, Ma'am. But I'm afraid we don't know who you are." He exchanged glances with Raine.

"Oh?" The woman raised her eyebrows.

"Yes, Ma'am. Paul sent me a message to come here, but don't know why." Raine was starting to feel as confused a the elderly woman now looked.

"Well, I'm Violet Fornell," the woman said, as if that ex plained everything.

"Show her the note, Raine," Ben said.

After Violet read the water-stained note that Raine had decoded, they explained to her how it had come to Raine Violet's look of puzzlement cleared slightly.

"So you see, Mrs. Fornell, we don't know exactly why Pau sent us here. We were assuming you would clear that up fo us," Raine said.

Violet nodded, absently stroking a calico cat that slept in he lap. "How long has it been since you've seen your husband dear?"

Raine blanched. "Paul is my brother, not my husband, Mrs Fornell," she explained, glancing at Ben. His eyes seemed to harden into blue glaciers as he stared back at her.

"Oh dear! I can't imagine why Paul. . .but now that I look at you, I see you resemble him quite—"

"Did Paul ever actually say that Raine was his wife?" Ben interrupted.

Violet stared at him thoughtfully. "Well, I. . .no, I guess he didn't. Not in so many words. But I just assumed from the way he talked about her. . ." Her words trailed off as she looked from Ben to Raine.

"We're just as confused as you are, Mrs. Fornell," Raine said, still looking at Ben. "It seems that Paul led a number of people to believe that he and I were something other than brother and sister."

Avoiding Raine's eyes, Ben spoke to Violet. "When was the last time you saw Paul, Mrs. Fornell?"

"Please, call me Violet." She peered at him over her glasses "I don't know what's going on here, but I can tell you all I know. I last saw Paul about three years ago after that ship of his sank, and. . ."

"You saw him after the *Aramathea* sank?" Raine's voice was eager.

"Why, yes. He lived here." Violet was clearly perplexed.

"But. . ." Raine tried to compose her thoughts.

"He didn't stay very long once he was well, but before he left, he gave me the key and told me to expect you, Raine."

"What do you mean, once he was well?" Raine's voice came out in a whisper.

"Well, my dear! Your brother had quite a time of it when the ship sank. He had to be in bed for quite awhile until that nasty gash healed properly, you know." Violet looked from Raine's pale face to the look of disbelief on Ben's. "Surely you knew. . ."

Raine shook her head.

"Oh dear. I better start at the beginning," Violet sighed. "Paul came to board with me shortly after he arrived here from England, I believe. I got to know him. . .quite well. In fact, he is very dear to me." Violet dabbed at her eyes with a lacy handkerchief. "I always prayed for his protection when he was on a voyage, but that last time was very unusual."

"Unusual?" Raine moved a large fern so she could draw her chair close to Violet's. Ben stood, his arms folded, his face tense.

"Yes. I had been concerned for him for some time. His soul, you know."

Raine nodded. Yes, she knew too well.

"He was such a bitter, hurting young man." Violet stared out the window. "Yet at the same time I knew his heart was still tender."

"But the voyage?" Ben prompted.

"Ah yes, the voyage." Violet smiled a faraway smile. "To make a long story short, I begged him not to go. I just felt in my spirit that he was not to go; that there was danger awaiting him. The Lord and I are on pretty good terms, you see." Her face shone with that special glow that comes only from an intimate walk with one's Savior.

Raine nodded, sensing the presence of the Spirit in this woman.

"Anyway, Paul wouldn't hear of missing that voyage."

Violet sighed and glanced at her visitors. "I couldn't stop him. But I prayed for him. Oh, how I prayed. One night, after Paul had been gone two weeks or so," Violet continued, "I was awakened in the middle of the night. I knew it was the time of crisis. I begged God for Paul's life, pleaded for his soul."

"What day was that, Violet?" Ben's face was pale.

"I believe it was the twenty-eighth of February, around two A.M."

Ben dropped to his knees in front of her chair. "That's the day she sank," he whispered.

Raine shook her head in wonder. "Thank You, God," she breathed. The room was silent then, the gentle Spirit of God whispering to three listening hearts as rain pattered softly on the window pane.

Two cups of Earl Grey later, Violet was refreshed enough to finish her story. Raine gasped as Violet described Paul coming home late one night, his head and face swathed in bandages. *Oh, Paul,* she groaned inwardly. *What happened that terrible night?*

"I made sure he rested properly. The poor boy was nearly starved." Violet said. "But as soon as he was well enough to get about on his own, he packed his bags." The elderly woman closed her eyes, obviously picturing the young man she loved as a son.

"The last thing Paul did before he left was to give me the key," Violet said quietly. "Hand me that box, dear." She indicated a polished brass box on the mantle. Opening it, she drew out a small key and reverently handed it to Raine.

Raine took the key with a trembling hand. "But what is it for?"

"I thought you would know what it was for, Raine." The older woman's face was troubled.

Raine handed the key to Ben, who examined it carefully, then slipped it into his pocket. He leaned over and kissed Violet's cheek. "We'll let you know as soon as we find out anything."

Violet nodded. "You do that."

Raine put her arms around the invalid's shoulders. "Thank you," she whispered.

Violet put an age-softened hand on Raine's cheek. "Our God is a great God, dear. Don't ever forget that."

Raine followed Ben out to the carriage, feeling a strange yearning. What would it take to be that close to God?

The ride home through the misting rain was silent, each wrapped in their own thoughts.

❧

Three days went by before Ben was free to visit Raine again. They were sitting on the porch swing, the cool summer breeze teasing them with the scent of roses.

"Would you pray for me, Raine?"

She glanced at him. "I've never stopped."

He took her hand, gently tracing the backs of her fingers. "I don't know what's wrong with me. I want to have a relationship with Christ, but I can't seem to get past the fear."

She was silent, giving him time to give voice to his thoughts. At last he continued, his voice heavy. "Also, I think we'd better not see each other any more." There. He'd said it. He felt her shock as she pulled her hand away to stare at him.

"Why?"

This was much harder than he imagined. "Because. . . because I need some time to think."

"Oh." The pain in her beautiful eyes made his stomach hurt. But what else could he do? He couldn't go on not knowing. . .

Her soft voice interrupted his thoughts. "Can't you tell me what's wrong, Ben?"

He couldn't bring himself to look at her.

"Ben?" She felt him touch his arm tentatively and he turned to her then.

"How do I know that it's not true, Raine?"

"What's not true?" Her face clouded at the coldness in his voice.

"How do I know that you aren't really married to Paul, and you're not just playing a game with me?"

She simply stared at him, as though too stunned to speak. "I've told you the truth, Ben," she said quietly at last. "If you don't trust me, then I guess there's nothing left for us."

She stood, and he almost gave in as he caught a faint whiff of her freshly-washed hair. He reached for her, then turned away.

"Good-bye, Raine," he said over his shoulder.

He saw her raise her hand as if to touch him, and then she wrapped her arms around herself as if to ward of a sudden chill. He couldn't bare to look at her any longer, and he quickly strode away and climbed into the carriage. He turned the horses and never once looked back.

If he had, he would have seen the tears streaming down Raine's face as she stumbled into the house, not caring who saw her misery.

"Why, Raine! What's wrong, child?" Her aunt's sympathetic voice only caused the tears to flow faster. She poured out the story, Aunt Grace clucking and sighing at the appropriate times.

"Why don't men have more sense!" Grace was thoroughly indignant by the time Raine had calmed down. "I have a mind to. . ."

"Now, now Gracie. I'm sure the boy will come to his senses." Uncle John had come into the room in time to hear Raine's tearful recounting of the evening. "Captain Ben won't be able to stay away for very long, if I know him."

"But why. . ."

"Raine, Ben loves you." John smiled at the look on his niece's face. "But men are funny sometimes. Loving you makes Ben vulnerable, and the way the situation looks to him, he thinks he's going to end up getting hurt. Just be patient, honey. He'll come around." Uncle John patted her hand. "A few prayers wouldn't hurt, either."

Raine plodded upstairs, somehow feeling like a lost little girl. Her heart hurt as she recalled the look on Ben's face. *Ben, I love you so much. How could you ask me to pray for you—and then doubt me?*

A quiet voice seemed to interrupt her anguish, saying, *And how could you doubt Me?* Raine slipped to her knees. *Please forgive me, Father God,* she cried. *I love Ben so much, but I want Your will to be done in my life. Please lead me in Your path.*

❧

The next day a letter from Constance arrived, bringing a smile in the midst of Raine's pain.

> *Dear Raine,*
> *You would never believe it! I have decided to stay here on the island! There are so many suffering people coming through these gates. My heart especially goes out to my Orthodox brothers and sisters, who are almost starving to death by the time they reach Ellis. You see, they only eat kosher foods, and no one seems to take notice of their special needs.*
> *Some of the Jewish workers here and myself are thinking of creating some sort of organization to help the Jewish immigrants. Not only with food, but with anything they need to get them established here in America. And if I get the chance, I'm not going to be afraid to tell them about the Messiah.*
> *Anyway, God is good. Thank you so much, dear, for leading me back to Him. I trust this letter finds you well. Kiss that handsome Captain Thackeray for me.*
>
> *Sincerely,*
> *Constance Rabinowicz*
>
> *P.S. I TOLD them I didn't have tuberculosis.*

I would certainly kiss Ben if he would come back to me, Raine thought mournfully. The dull ache in her heart would not go away. Tired of sitting around the house the last few days, she finally asked Uncle John to drive her to Violet's house. *Maybe she thought of something else helpful,* Raine hoped. In any case, it would be delightful to spend some time with the cheery woman.

"I'll be back in an hour, Raine," Uncle John called as he dropped her off at Violet's door.

Violet was delighted to see Raine, tactfully refraining from asking about Ben when she noticed the sad look in Raine's emerald eyes.

"Would you mind pouring?" she asked instead, handing Raine the flowered teapot.

Thoroughly enjoying the older woman's company, Raine glanced at the clock in surprise when Uncle John knocked on the door. Could an hour have passed so quickly?

"Come in and meet Violet," she suggested as she let him in.

Uncle John obligingly stepped into the sunny room, stopping short as he recognized the woman in the wheelchair. "Well—"

"Hello, John!" Violet interrupted. "This is a surprise!"

Raine looked from Violet to her Uncle John. "You two know each other?"

Her uncle looked distinctly uncomfortable. "Yes. We knew each other back in London, Raine." He looked at Violet. "I had no idea you had moved here to Boston."

"I wasn't aware that you and Grace lived in Boston either, John." Violet's eyes were steady as she gazed at him.

"Yes, well." John cleared his throat nervously. "It was nice seeing you again. I'll be sure to tell Grace." He turned to Raine. "We'd better get going, Raine."

Raine wasn't quite sure what was going on, but there was no mistaking the undercurrent of tension. "I'll come visit again soon, Violet," she promised.

"I'll look forward to it, dear."

"What was that all about, Uncle John?" Raine asked as soon as they were out the door.

John didn't answer until they were out of sight of Violet's house. "I'm sorry if I seemed rude, Raine. It was quite a shock to see an old acquaintance from England after all this time," he said slowly. Raine looked at him questioningly, certain he was not telling her everything.

She was surprised to see a carriage in the drive as they pulled up to Uncle John's house.

"Well Raine, it looks like your captain is back!" John seemed glad for the diversion from his thoughts.

She stepped down from the carriage, her heart pounding. Walking slowly to the front door, she failed to see Ben as he stood in the shade of the old oak.

ॐ

Ben's mouth went dry as he saw her. She looked like a breath of spring, the plumes of her hat exactly matching the peacock blue of her dress. *I've been such a fool,* he thought. *God, please let her forgive me...*

"Raine!" She whirled, her eyes wide, and he approached her slowly, as one would approach a frightened animal. Finally standing in front of her, he searched her face. "Can you forgive me?" he asked in a low voice.

He watched the joy leap into her eyes. "Yes," she said simply.

"I've been miserable without you, Raine. I love you." He pulled her into his embrace. He felt her smile against his chest, and although he couldn't be sure, he thought he heard her whisper, "I love you too."

"I missed you so much." Suddenly remembering something, he dug into his pocket. He folded her gloved hand around the key. "I've been thinking a lot about what you said about trust. I don't know what this key belongs to, Raine, but I know that I can trust you with the key to my heart. I was wrong to doubt you."

She looked up at him, her eyes shining. "I..."

"Well, now. Here's the good captain!" Uncle John clapped Ben on the shoulder.

Raine sighed. Uncle John had a way of choosing the most inopportune moments...

After supper, Grace laid the small brass key on the table, studying it intently. "I don't know for sure, but I would guess that this key would open a safety deposit box," she ventured.

"Of course!" Ben was elated. All four of them had been

mulling over the various unanswered questions regarding Paul, trying to figure out the significance of the key.

Raine's heart soared, then sank. "We could spend months trying to find the right bank." Everyone was silent. *Have we come this far only to reach a dead end?* Raine wondered.

"I think we ought to pay a visit to Violet again," Ben announced suddenly. "Didn't she say that she had Paul run errands for her sometimes? Maybe she knows what bank he would have gone to."

❧

"Yes," Violet nodded. "Paul often went to the bank for me. I use the one down on First Street."

"Sounds like a good place to start," Ben said.

Violet reached for both of their hands. "God go with you," she said fervently. "Please let me know when you find my boy."

Raine felt tears prick the backs of her eyelids. "We will, Violet. We will."

❧

El Paso County, Colorado

The Crooked P ranch hands were working furiously. The rain had finally stopped and they had to make up for lost time. Tom worked alongside his men, readying ten head of cattle for the trip south to Santa Fe.

Laying aside the branding iron, Tom wiped the sweat from his face. Stuffing his bandanna into his pocket, he ambled over to the well where several of the hands were gathered. He dipped himself a cool drink from the full bucket that stood nearby, then sank wearily to the ground.

"Only 'bout a dozen of them ornery creatures left, Boss." Simon nodded toward the holding pen.

Tom nodded, then entered the log ranch house, throwing his sweaty shirt on the floor. Passing the fireplace, his eye caught sight of the Bible on the shelf where he had left it that rainy day. His soul reached out for it, but his mind would not obey. Turning his head, he walked away.

Two days later, he pulled his bandanna up over his face. "Let's get going, boys!"

The excitement of a cattle drive always did wonders for him, and he'd been especially looking forward to this trip to Santa Fe. Maybe he could leave the torment of his past for a few days. What he wouldn't give. . .

five

Raine drew a deep breath as the teller directed her and Ben into a small room. Ben couldn't believe how easy it had been to find the right bank. The teller had taken one look at the key, asked Raine her name, and that was that.

Now, he set the long metal box on the table with a thunk. "Take as much time as you need."

Raine fitted the key into the lock with shaking fingers. *Will she at last find the answers to all of her questions?* Ben wondered. She looked up at him, and he smiled encouragingly. He was sure that they had been followed to the bank, but now was not the time to tell her that.

He frowned, remembering the face of the red-haired man that had been behind them all morning. He was sure it was the same man he had seen that time outside his office back in London. The face had seemed familiar somehow, not only because he had seen the man that other time but as though he should have known the man's name, as though he'd known him from some other place and time. . . "Go ahead," he encouraged her. He found himself holding his breath, distracted from his thoughts, and, for the time being, he forgot about the red-haired man.

She opened the lid slowly. Peering over her shoulder, Ben was surprised to see that it contained only two envelopes. As she picked up the largest one first, he noticed that Paul's handwriting was very sloppy, as if he had written Raine's name in haste.

Taking a deep breath, she slid the contents out. She glanced at the inner envelope, then held it out to Ben so he could see the note scrawled across it. *Raine, please get this into the hands of Ben Thackeray.* He almost grabbed it out of her hands.

He ripped it open, heaving a huge sigh of relief as he glimpsed the contents. He had hoped against hope that it would turn out to be something like this.

"What is it?"

He glanced up at her, regret momentarily covering the joy in his eyes. "I'm sorry, Raine. I'm not at liberty to share this information with you yet. There's something I need to do first."

Her eyes widened.

"But I can tell you one thing—this is wonderful news!" He caught her up suddenly and whirled her around in the air.

"Put me down," she pleaded with a giggle.

He did so at once, standing back to admire her. What a picture she was. Her hat had fallen off, revealing the gorgeous mass of dark curls. Her cheeks were pink from laughter, and her mouth. . . He pulled her to him, no longer able to resist. Her lips felt soft beneath his as they yielded to the hungry pressure of his own. "Ah, Raine," he whispered. "What have you done to me?"

He released her after a long moment, watching as she picked up the envelope that still lay in the box. She stared at the date that Paul had penciled in under her name. *February 1, 1903* "This was right before the *Aramathea* set sail," she whispered.

She slid a single sheet of paper out of the envelope. Yellowed with age and dog-eared, it seemed to be some sort of legal document. She stared at it uncomprehendingly for a moment, then gasped as she realized what she was holding. How could it be?

Ben took the paper from her shaking hand. He scanned the few words it contained, then shrugged as he looked up at her.

She pointed to a line on the birth certificate that stated a women named Miriam was Paul's natural mother. "My mother's name was Ellen."

"Ah." Comprehension dawned on him as he reread it. "I'm sorry, Raine."

"So am I." Her lips were pressed together in a tight line. "I'm sure this is most of the reason Paul never came back, even to see me." Slipping it back into the envelope, she stooped to pick up a single sheet of paper that had fallen to the floor, then held it so they both could read it.

Dear Raine,
I have missed you so! Has Papa poisoned you against
me so much that you won't even answer one of my letters?

Ben saw her eyes fill with tears, and he knew her heart was
breaking at the thought that Paul might think she had aban-
doned him.

Perhaps Papa has forbade you to have contact with
me? I can only hope that you have not forgotten me com-
pletely. I'm sure you can see why I will never come home
—not until Ben follows the directions I've left him and lets
me know the results. I don't have time to write you every-
thing that happened, but I trust that since you have gotten
this far, that Ben has told you as much as he could. I am in
danger, and I fear that you would be in danger also if you
were with me. But how I long for your sweet company!

The tears were flowing freely down her face as she read the
last sentences out loud. "Please, Raine. If you can't find it in
your heart to write to me, at least pray for me. Please pray for
me, little sister."

Ben gathered her into his arms, rocking her gently. He
could tell that all the pent-up emotion of the last weeks
flowed out with her tears, soaking the front of his shirt. "Shh,
it's going to be fine," he murmured comfortingly. "I'm right
here, Raine. . .I love you."

She laid her head on his shoulder.

&

"So where do you go from here, Raine?" Uncle John had just
finished reading Paul's letter.

"I don't know." She wrinkled her brow. "I just can't figure
out why I haven't received any letters from Paul. Apparently
he thinks I know where he is."

"Do you think he could still be here in Boston, Raine?"

"No, I don't think so, Aunt Grace. There was no date on the
letter, but somehow I feel that it was written quite a while ago."
She smiled suddenly. "I do know that God has led me this far

It looks like a dead end, but I know He can work it out."

"Especially since *He* knows where Paul is, even though we don't," her uncle reminded her. "What does Ben think?"

"I guess he's as puzzled as I am," she admitted. "Although there was something in that other envelope he can't tell me about yet."

She bid her aunt and uncle good night and closed the door to her room with a sigh of relief. The events of the day paraded through her mind as she knelt down by the bed. She was horrified anew at the indisputable truth that the old document had brought to light.

Papa, how could you? her heart cried.

I love you, Raine. Ben's words of love comforted her again as she remembered the warmth of his embrace. She buried her face in her pillow. *I need to talk to You, Father. I know You've led me this far, but I don't know where to go next. Please lead me. . .*

She awoke the next morning feeling refreshed and at peace, but no closer to knowing what to do next. The cool morning air beckoned to her irresistibly. Letting herself out the front door without a sound, she took a long walk. She breathed in the freshness of the beautiful morning, and somehow it gave her courage to face the dawning of the new day.

"Good morning," she sang cheerfully as she entered the kitchen door.

The look on her aunt's face made her heart stop. "What's wrong?" she whispered.

"Your father—" Grace handed her a telegram. "This just came, dear."

Raine read the short message, its words chilling her soul.

RICHARD THOMAS VERY ILL STOP PLEASE COME
QUICKLY STOP PASSAGE BOOKED ON THE
CORNUCOPIA *STOP AUGUST 15 STOP*

The telegram was signed by Dr. Delfin, an old family friend.

"August 15th? That's tomorrow!" She was stunned. "I need to pack and. . ."

"Slow down there, Raine." Uncle John's hand on her shoulder was gentle. "You'll have plenty of time."

"Oh, Uncle John. What if Papa dies before I get there?" She had discovered in the past few seconds how much she loved her father, despite her anger with him.

"We'll pray that God will keep him until you have a chance to see him, Raine." John's voice was firm. "God is able."

"I know, Uncle John. It's just that Papa and I have been at odds ever since Paul left, and I don't want him to die until we can make it right." She bowed her head. "I've been so angry with him," she whispered. "I keep asking God to help me forgive, but just when I think I have, I find myself bitter again."

"Forgiveness is a process," John reminded her. "As long as you want to forgive, and you keep working at it, it will come."

&

"I'm so sorry I can't go with you back to England, Raine." As they stood by the *Cornucopia* the next day, Ben felt as though a weight was about to settle on his shoulders. "I wish I wasn't obligated to stay in Boston for at least a few more weeks."

"I'll be fine, Ben. But I will miss you terribly." Her eyes filled with tears. "When will I see you again?"

He enfolded her in his arms. "Don't cry, honey. We'll be together again soon, I promise. In the meantime, I'll try to track down that brother of yours. I'd like to talk to him before I take care of that matter he left for me to do."

He kissed her tenderly, then gave her a gentle nudge toward the gangway. Pressing a small package into her hand, he looked deep into her eyes. "I love you, Raine."

She kissed him swiftly on his cheek, then turned to go.

He watched until the ship was no longer in sight. *I miss her already,* he thought, a strange sense of foreboding coming over him as he climbed into the carriage. *Don't be silly, old chap. Nothing is going to happen to her.* Nevertheless, he felt a heaviness that he couldn't seem to shake. The sinister face of the red-haired man popped into his mind and suddenly, finally, he was able to put a name with the face.

Dag. Dagmar Rennet. Ever since Ben had seem him, he

had been trying to remember why his face seemed so familiar. Now he knew, and it chilled him to the bone. Why, oh why hadn't he gone with her?

Then again, maybe it was himself that Dag was after. After all, Paul had left the other envelope for Ben, not Raine. The thought was not a pleasant one, but at least it was better him than Raine.

His mind occupied with matters besides his driving, he was surprised when he realized he was driving down High Street, where Paul used to live. *I'll visit Violet,* he decided, smiling at the thought of the cheery old woman.

Nearing her house, the tiny seed of an idea that he had been contemplating suddenly bloomed. Pulling the horses to an abrupt stop, he marched up to Violet's door and knocked with conviction. He entered when he heard Violet's welcome float from somewhere within."

"Good morning, Violet."

"Ben! What brings you here? Did you find Paul already?" Her voice was eager.

"No, I'm afraid not, Violet. But I was wondering. . ."

"Yes?"

"Could I stay here for a while?"

She was startled. "Well, I. . .I haven't had any boarders since Paul. . ."

"It wouldn't be for very long," he said persuasively. "Probably a month or two."

She looked him over. "You aren't in trouble with the law or anything, are you?"

He laughed. "No, Ma'am." He explained about Raine's abrupt departure for England.

She closed her eyes. "I hope Raine gets to see her father before he dies." She smiled at him suddenly. "You know, it does get lonely here sometimes. Do you play chess?"

❧

The weather during the voyage back to London was unseasonably stormy and cold, emphasizing the contrast between this voyage and her experience aboard the *Capernaum*. Raine stayed in her cabin, nibbling on bread in an effort to keep her stomach on an even keel. She spent much of her time in prayer, not knowing what to expect when she arrived at her father's home.

At last, after many long days, the skyline of London came into view through the thick fog. Raine stood on deck, pensively fingering the small key that hung around her neck with Paul's locket. She had discovered the tiny key when she had opened the package from Ben.

> *Dear Raine,*
> *This is just to remind you that you hold the key to my heart. Come back to me soon.*
>
> > *All my love,*
> > *Ben*

His words of love warmed her as the *Cornucopia* steamed into the harbor. Scanning the crowded wharf, Raine's heart leapt as she saw a dark-haired man standing near the front of the crowd.

Paul! Her mind screamed. Grasping her bag tightly, she kept her eyes glued on the man as the ship moved closer. Disappointment flooded over her as she saw that it wasn't her brother.

Sighing, she realized that her knuckles were turning white from the grip she had on her bag. Setting it down, she leaned against the railing. *Father, please calm my spirit,* she prayed.

There had been no mention in the telegram of anyone meeting Raine in London, so she made her way to the Mission.

Mr. Duncan thought he had seen the last of me, I'm sure, she thought in amusement. Walking slowly, she reflected on all that had happened since she left London.

Deep in thought, she was startled when a small group of children joyfully accosted her.

"Miss Thomas, Miss Thomas!"

"Did you come back to be our teacher?"

"Did you miss us?"

Raine gave each little one a hug. "I'm afraid I can only stay for a little while, children," she said regretfully. Their disappointed little faces tugged at her heart, making her realize how much she had missed teaching them.

"Charlotte!" Raine felt a rush of joy at seeing her old friend.

"Raine!" Charlotte gave her a huge hug. "Where did you come from?"

"I thought I'd just drop by and see you since I missed you so much."

Charlotte raised her eyebrows. "Mmm-hmm. Why are you really here? Oh dear, did things not work out with Captain Bert?"

"Ben. No actually, it's my father. Apparently he's very ill. Do you suppose Mr. Duncan would put up too much of a fuss if I spent the night here, just tonight?"

Charlotte shrugged. "You're my guest. If he doesn't like it, then that's his problem."

Raine pushed open the door of her old room, weary beyond belief. It would feel wonderful to have a good night's sleep before facing the ordeal tomorrow. She set the candle on the old dresser, groaning as she saw the piles of boxes on top of the bed. Apparently this was now the storage room.

Finally snuggled under the dusty coverlet, she tried to sleep. What was Ben doing right now? She could picture him standing at the railing of the *Capernaum* and wished she were with him.

Forcing her thoughts away from Ben, she thought of her father. *God, please let him live until I can get there,* she prayed once again. *Please give me the grace to forgive him. I can't do it on my own. And take care of Ben and Paul, please Father,* she continued. *They both need Your love. . .*

The knock on the door startled her awake. "It's just me," she heard Charlotte whisper.

"Do you realize it's one o'clock in the morning?" Raine opened one eye to glare at her friend.

"I know. But I forgot to ask you if that man found you."

Raine made a very unladylike noise. "What are you talking about, Charlotte?"

"A few weeks after you left, a man came looking for you.

He said he was your neighbor or something."

"My neighbor?" What neighbor? Surely this could have waited until morning.

"Well, I just thought it might be something important. I'll let you get back to your beauty sleep." Charlotte sounded hurt.

"Wait, Char." A faint alarm went off somewhere in the back of her mind. "What did he look like?"

"Well, he had blond hair, and his face was. . .well, it was very badly scarred."

Raine's throat constricted. "What did you tell him?" she whispered.

Charlotte shrugged. "Just that you had gone to America. Oh, and that you sailed on the *Capernaum*. He seemed very nice," she added defensively.

Raine closed her eyes. "What was his name?"

"I knew you would ask me that. Let's see, it was something like George or Gregory maybe. . .that was it! Gregory Havner. I think."

She didn't know anyone named Gregory Havner. "Did he say what he wanted?"

"No. . .maybe his name was Guthrie. Guthrie Havner? No, no! It was Geoffrey. Yes, I'm sure of it."

"Geoffrey?" The only Geoffrey she had ever know was Geoff Hathaway, her brother's old friend. But it couldn't be him. He was dead, killed in the fire that had destroyed his family's house. She pictured the disfigured face of the man who had called to her that day in Boston. Could it be. . .? Even at the time, she had had to admit that there was something familiar about him. But it couldn't be Geoff.

"Was it Geoffrey Hathaway?"

"Yes! Yes! That was it!" Charlotte bounced up and down on the bed. "So you do know him."

"Yes," Raine said slowly. "Except he's—dead." She remembered again the man's scars. Could it be possible that he had lived. . .? And why would he be trying to find her?

It was a very long time before she gave her body the sleep it was craving.

six

Ben scanned the room that had been Paul's and was now his. *If I were Paul, where would I hide something important?* He had come to stay at Violet's house with the general idea of gleaning more information about Paul's disappearance, but now a plan was beginning to formulate in his mind.

"There must be something obvious that we're missing," he mused out loud. *God, please help me to. . .*

He stopped short, realizing what he was doing. He had gotten so accustomed to Raine praying about everything.

Could it be this easy? Could he have a relationship with God like Raine and her uncle had? They made it sound so natural, talking to God as if He were really interested. Remembering the peace and joy that lighted Raine's beautiful eyes, his yearning suddenly grew undeniable. Falling to his knees in the middle of Paul's room, he cried out, "Jesus, if You really do care, please show me the way to You. I can't live without peace any more. . ."

Across the ocean, Raine sat bolt upright in bed. The urge to pray for Ben was so strong, she got out of bed and knelt down. Pleading first for his safety, she soon found herself praying that he would be able to surrender himself to God.

Finally feeling a peace come over her as the first glow of dawn peeked through the darkness, she got up and got dressed. Between the excitement of Charlotte's middle-of-the-night revelations and the prayers for Ben, she hadn't gotten much sleep. Oh, well. She could rest on the train on the way to St. Albans.

Digging her Bible out of the small overnight bag, she settled by the still-dark window. The train didn't leave for several more hours, but her stomach felt tight already, just thinking about seeing her father. She leaned back in her chair to watch the slowly-rising sun, relaxing in spite of herself. Opening her Bible, she tensed as she heard a slight sound at her door. She stared in horrified fascination as the door knob turned. The door opened slowly, soundlessly. She froze, clutching her Bible to her chest.

The large, red-haired man looked startled to see her awake, then an ugly smile creased his face. "So—we finally meet, Raine Oliver."

She opened her mouth to scream, but he was too fast. Clamping a grimy hand over her mouth, he pulled her back against his chest. "Now, don't make a sound, or you'll never see the light of day again," he threatened quietly. "We're going to go for a ride, and I don't want to hear one noise out of you. Do you understand?"

She nodded.

The man loosened his grip a hair. "If you cooperate, you won't get hurt," he said, watching her intently.

She nodded again.

He opened his coat slightly, revealing a wicked-looking knife. "Now, you're going to walk down the stairs and get into my carriage."

Oh, I am, am I? She gritted her teeth.

He whipped her around to face him as he felt her body tense. "You'd better not try anything, do you understand?" He prodded her out the door, almost stepping on the hem of her dress as he followed her.

God, please let someone see us, she pleaded silently as she made her way down the stairs. She walked as slowly as possible, stalling for time.

Passing Mr. Duncan's study, her heart leapt as she saw a crack of light under the door. Pretending to stumble, she slammed against the door. *Come on, Mr. Duncan.* The man behind her jerked her up. He gave her a shove, cursing under his breath.

Raine glanced back at Mr. Duncan's door, her hopes dashed when it remained closed. Her captor hustled her into a windowless carriage. Jumping in after her, he motioned to the waiting driver. The carriage started with a jolt as the horses leapt forward.

She glared at the red-haired man, mildly surprised that he wasn't Geoff, or whoever was pretending to be Geoff. Maybe this big lug was in cahoots with scar-face Geoff. That must be it.

"What do you want with me?" she demanded.

"Well, now. Ain't we the feisty one!" He chuckled.

She turned her back to him. His breath alone could kill her before he even got to her with the knife, she thought grimly. She wished she could see where they were going. Judging from the many turns, she guessed that the driver was trying to disorient her.

The carriage stopped abruptly, almost throwing her to the floor. Before she realized what was happening, her captor whipped a scarf out of his pocket and tied it around her eyes. Fear threatened to overwhelm her as she was jerked from the carriage and forced to stumble along beside him.

The Lord is my shepherd, I shall not want. She felt her whole body begin to tremble violently, then the blackness closed in on her. She crumpled in a heap at her captor's feet.

❧

She came to slowly, knowing that she was on a ship even before she opened her eyes. The slight rocking motion and the damp, musty smell of the hold had penetrated her mind, even in her unconscious state. Reaching up, she pulled the filthy blindfold off, realizing as she did so that she was not alone.

Her captor sat perched on a crate, his leering smile barely visible in the faint light. "Well, I guess yer not so brave after all, are ya. Sure are purty, though."

She recoiled at his suggestive tone, shrinking back as he rose and came toward her.

He laughed, a horrible sound that sent chills down her spine. "I won't bother ya none, yet. We'll just see how ya feel about me after a day or two down here, Mrs. Oliver." He grinned nastily. "I'm sure you'll have plenty of company with all the rats and such."

She heard a key turn in the lock as he left, then the heavy thump of a dead bolt. Thankful at least that he had not tied her up, she moved to sit on top of a large box. Pulling her feet up securely underneath her, she pondered her situation. *What does this man want with me? He apparently thinks I'm someone else,* she thought, wondering why he seemed to think her last name was Oliver. Oliver. . .Oliver. . .that sounded so familiar. Suddenly she knew, and she groaned out loud. *Paul.* Paul had gone by the name Paul Oliver when he was sailing. And this man had called her Mrs. Oliver!

Apparently he too thought she and Paul were married. Unable to make any sense of the situation, she stood up to explore her prison. Feeling her way around, she discovered many boxes and barrels, but no way of escape.

Settling herself on a bale of something soft, she tried to devise a plan of escape, but the loud growling of her stomach kept distracting her. The scones she had eaten for supper last night were long gone. Her fear was fast turning into anger the longer she sat in the dark. Determined to find a way out, she jumped down from her perch.

"Ouch!" Her foot landed on something soft and warm that squeaked. She scrambled back up on top of the crates, her stomach threatening to expel its meager contents. At least he was truthful about the rats!

"Why didn't I beg you to come with me, Ben?" She groaned. "Now what am I going to do? I can't sit on this crate for the rest of my life."

Closing her eyes, she concentrated on Ben, remembering his smile, his touch. Her thoughts drifting, she gasped as she realized that her father would be expecting her today. *If he's still alive,* her mind whispered. She pushed that thought aside, hoping instead that her disappearance would be noticed quickly. *Father God, please send someone soon!*

❧

Several days later, heavy footfalls paused at the door. Raine jumped up from where she had been lying. The door had been opened only twice since she had been put there, once for a loaf of bread to be tossed in, and once for a bucket of water to be carelessly pushed through.

Her heart beat faster as the heavy door flew open. Shielding her eyes from the sudden glare of a candle, she felt her mouth go dry. Her captor loomed over her, a heavy rope in his hand.

"Did ya have a nice stay, Mrs. Oliver?" The large man was clearly amused by the situation.

Raine glared at him and he chuckled. Suddenly, his hand snaked out and grasped her wrist in an iron grip. "I certainly hope that ya feel like talking to me, sweetheart," he growled, "because I'm not a very patient man. I've waited too long as it is."

Raine stared numbly at her hand as it turned white from the force of his grip on her wrist. Her lack of response infuriated him. Jerking her around, he tied her hands together roughly. He prodded her out of the hold, forcing her up the stairs and into a small, brightly lit cabin.

Seeing her captor's face clearly now, she shuddered at the evil gleam in his eye. She kept her eyes averted as he tied her in a chair. He gently ran his fingers through her dark hair, then began to pace in front of her.

"Where are they?" He demanded finally.

She stared at him. *Where is who?*

"Answer me, woman! Where are those papers?"

Papers? Father, please help me! She met her captor's frenzied look with a steady gaze.

"I don't know what papers you're talking about."

He roared an oath. "Don't play innocent with me. I followed you and your lover to the bank. I know what you went there for."

She jumped as his huge fist crashed into the wall next to her. The papers that had been in the safety deposit box, of course. The ones she had never read.

Closing her eyes, she fully expected to feel the next blow on her face. After a moment, she cautiously opened her eyes.

He stood in front of her, visibly trembling, but under control.

"Come now, sweetheart. I won't hurt you." His voice was unexpectedly calm. "Just give me the papers."

She eyed him warily. "I think you've got the wrong person," she said. "I don't have any papers. Truly. And my last name is Thomas, not Oliver."

"Oh? Then how d'ya explain this?"

She gasped as he whipped a large photograph from his pocket. The picture was tattered and water-stained, but there was no mistaking it.

It was the picture that Raine had given to Paul before he left home. But hadn't Paul given the picture to Ben? Surely Ben isn't involved in this. . . She pushed the ugly thought from her mind.

"Where did you get that?" she whispered.

He looked smug. "You don't need to know, sweetheart."

The endearment coming from this man's lips made her cringe.

"Shall I refresh your memory as to what is written on the back of this purty little photo?" he continued mockingly. "To Paul—my one and only. Love, Raine Ellen."

She sighed. How could this get so twisted? If only Paul could explain. . .

"So, where is your husband?" The question jolted Raine, even though she knew it was coming.

"I don't have a husband." She was shocked at how firm her voice sounded.

Her captor looked stunned for a moment, but recovered quickly. "You mean Paul is dead?" he asked, the nasty gleam coming back into his eye. "Don't play games with me, woman. Tell me where he is."

Raine looked him in the eye. "I don't know."

Red Hair kicked the leg of the chair, sending her to the floor, the chair on top of her. Letting loose a string of profanity like she'd never heard before, he untied her and bodily carried her back down to the hold. Forcing her inside, he slammed the door closed.

"You will tell me sooner or later, little woman, so you might as well make it sooner. I'm going to get those papers, wherever they are. And then I'm going to get Paul."

Hearing the bolt thump into place, she sank trembling to the floor. *God, help me.*

❧

"Well, Captain." John looked at his Bible thoughtfully. "You just keep reading this Book and keep asking Him to teach you His ways. He'll show you."

Ben couldn't believe the joy and peace that he had known since he finally surrendered all to the Lord. After puzzling over some Scriptures for days, he had finally sought the wisdom of Raine's uncle.

"Thanks, John." Ben got up to leave, pausing at the door. "Have you heard from Raine yet?"

John shook his head, a troubled light in his eye. "No. I expected that she would have arrived in London two days ago. She said she would send a telegram when she arrived in St. Albans, apprising us of her father's condition. It's just not like her to go back on her word."

I knew I should have gone with her. Ben felt a heavy foreboding drop on him like a cloak.

"I don't like it, John," he said out loud, images of Dag filling his mind "I don't like it at all."

Raine's uncle nodded in agreement. "I know what you mean, son. I don't have a good feeling about it either. I think. . ." His voice trailed off at the look on Ben's face. "What is it, Captain?"

Ben swallowed hard. Surely it couldn't be, yet. . . "Do you think it's possible that the telegram from Raine's father was a hoax?"

John started visibly. "What are you getting at?"

"I'm afraid someone has been following her."

"Someone?"

Ben sighed. "It's a very long story, John, and I think Paul is right in the middle of it."

"Go on."

"I think it first began before Paul even left England. Have you heard how he and a friend of his found that old code book?"

"Raine alluded to it, yes."

"It seems that code book belonged to a group of spies. They were gathering information from an insider in the British government, passing message's on to sailors bound for Africa, who in turn passed them along to the native rebels in South Africa. Their reward was South African diamonds.

"Paul stumbled onto their activities, apparently totally by accident, when one of his innocent code messages was intercepted by a member of the circle of spies. Needless to say, the spies were not happy that Paul knew about them—they were about to take action against him, when their insider in the government betrayed them.

"The government did a massive sweep, and caught most of the spies—and they almost caught Paul as well, mistaking the innocent message the spies had intercepted as the genuine article. It was all kept very hush-hush by the government, and Raine never even knew what was going on. But apparently, espionage was among the numerous other things Paul was accused of before he left St. Albans."

"What? And Raine knows nothing about that?"

"Not a clue." Ben gave a rueful grin. "I have to admit that for awhile I thought she was in on it."

John stared at him. "You knew about the espionage all along?"

Ben shook his head. "I didn't know any of this when I hired Paul. But it didn't take long for rumors to start flying."

John nodded, his face an unreadable mask.

"By that time, I had gotten to know Paul myself. I just couldn't quite believe he could do anything so underhanded. I decided not to say anything and just keep an eye on the situation. Then, just as the *Aramathea* left Boston on her last trip, one of my sailors came to me with what he said was evidence that Paul was a spy. He showed me a message that Paul had written in code, and said he had a friend in St. Albans who had

eard the whole story. He claimed he had seen Paul passing
ıformation to another sailor when we were in port."

"Did you believe him?"

Ben shifted in his chair. "I'll tell you, John, I didn't want
ɔ. And I didn't trust the fellow who told me the story. But
ιere was something about Paul, something that made me
ιink he wasn't quite telling me the truth. I kept hoping that
ɔmehow he could prove his innocence." He ran his fingers
ιrough his hair. "I had intended to confront him with the
ailor's story, but I never got the chance."

John raised his eyebrows.

"The ship sank before I had a chance to speak with him."

John blew out his breath. "This would break Raine's heart,
ou know."

Ben nodded. "I just couldn't tell her, yet."

"Wise. Do you still suspect Paul?"

Ben sighed. "I have. . .found evidence that has convinced
ιe that Paul was framed." As much as he wanted to, he just
ouldn't tell John yet about those papers in the safe deposit
ox. There was too much at stake. Soon he would have to
ct on the evidence the papers contained. If only he could
ιnd Paul first.

"What are you telling me, Captain?"

"I think that the man who framed Paul may have found out
ιat Paul is still alive and is trailing Raine to see if she will
ad him to Paul."

"But how. . ."

"I saw the man following us when we went to the bank that
ay," he admitted. He shook his head. "I only caught a
:limpse of his face, and I thought he looked familiar, but. . .
vho would've thought? It was the same sailor who told
ne the story about Paul being a spy in the first place. I'd give
ınything to go back and confront the man, demand he tell me
vhat he was up to—but I can't."

John's face was tight with anxiety. "Is this man dangerous?"

Ben shrugged. "I'd wager that anyone who can hold a
:rudge that long isn't playing a game."

John passed his hand over his face. "I'll get a telegram o
to Raine's father. In the meantime, it sounds like we better d
a whole lot of praying, Captain."

ta

Ben was waiting beside his carriage when John came hom
from the office the next day. John's demeanor gave the answe
to his unspoken question.

"I know something has happened to her, John!" The horse
jumped as he slammed his fist into the carriage door.

"Calm yourself, Ben," John said sharply. "Do you or d
you not believe that God will care for Raine?"

Ben stared at the older man. "I know He can take care c
her, John. It's just that I wish I were there to protect her, too.'

"I know, son." Raine's uncle looked weary. "But God ha
seen fit to do otherwise. Besides, Raine's a pretty strong ga
as I'm sure you know."

Ben nodded ruefully, remembering the steady light in he
eye as she had told him of her plans to travel to Boston alone
I'm not afraid, Ben. He could hear her voice like it wa
yesterday. *God, please protect her, wherever she is. . .*

ta

Near Santa Fe, New Mexico

Tom stared unseeingly at the backs of the cattle. Lifting hi
Stetson, he let the hot, dusty wind ruffle his hair and dry th
sweat from his brow.

It felt good to be on the trail again, free from the day-to-da
routine of the ranch, free from the daily strain of—waiting
Waiting for what, he wasn't sure, but he could feel th
expectancy growing daily. During the day he could push i
aside, but in the quiet of the night, it pulled at him, robbin
him of much-needed rest. At the same time, it brought with i
the hope of change; renewal. What was it? Why was his hear
reaching for it, yet holding back in fear?

seven

Richard Thomas stared at the telegram from his brother-in-law, trying to still the violent trembling of his hands.

RICHARD STOP HOPE YOU ARE FEELING BETTER
STOP PLEASE SEND NEWS OF RAINE'S ARRIVAL
STOP JOHN

The last sentence rang in his fevered mind. Devastated when she had not shown up, he had assumed his daughter had chosen not to come to him. "I can't die without seeing her." Burying his face in his hands, he wept bitter tears. *Please God, give me a chance.*

&

Raine lifted her head at the slight noise, then laid it down again. *It's your imagination,* she told herself. Her brain felt fuzzy, as if a fog had rolled in and encompassed her thoughts. Weak from hunger, she floated in and out of wakefulness.

"Raine!"

She jerked her head up at the loud whisper. "Ben?" Had he really come? "I'm over here."

"Raine, you need to get up!" His voice was urgent.

She stared groggily at him as he tried to rouse her. "You're not Ben," she said slowly. Maybe he was an angel? She had always wondered what angels looked like.

"Raine—if you want to get out of here, you need to listen to me." His voice was insistent.

Her brain felt frozen. Concentrating on his words, she sat up with effort.

"Raine, I'm sorry, but I need to cut your hair. It's the only way we'll be able to pull this off."

A faint alarm went off somewhere in her hazy thoughts, but

she couldn't figure out why. She squinted at him as he snipped her hair, trying to make sense of his features, but she couldn't think. . .couldn't concentrate. . . Why was she here. . .? She seemed to recognize the man, but no name came to her thoughts, no name that made sense. . . Her thoughts were clouded with hunger and confusion.

Her rescuer pushed some garments into her hands, then turned his back. "Get into those clothes, Raine," he commanded. "Hurry!"

She obediently stepped into the trousers, feeling an odd sense of detachment from the scene. He turned back around, sweeping her with a quick glance. "It'll have to do," he mumbled. Slapping a tattered cap on her head, he gathered her in his arms and bolted up the stairs. Her head bobbed against his shoulder as he made a dash across the open deck and out onto the crowded wharf. Slowing his pace abruptly, he put her on her feet.

"Raine—listen to me. You're going to be safe soon. But you need to walk. We'll draw too much attention if I have to carry you." His voice was pleading. "Can you do it?"

She looked into the man's eyes, gaining strength as the word *safe* penetrated her mind. She nodded.

੩ਡ

She opened her eyes. What time was it? Weakly, she pulled herself up in the bed.

Martha, the Mission's nurse sprang up from her chair by the window. "Raine! You're awake!"

"Why are you in my room?" Maybe one of the children was ill and they needed Raine to help. . .

"You've been, ah, sick, Raine," Martha's voice was hesitant. "You don't remember?"

Raine stared at the ceiling, trying to think. "I remember coming here from Boston, and. . ." From Boston! Instantly everything came flooding back. She had been kidnapped, then someone had rescued her, and. . .

"How did I get back here to the Mission, Martha?" she asked. This was too strange.

"I think I'd better have Mr. Duncan speak with you, Raine."

Raine grimaced. One of the last people she wanted to see. . .

The nurse laughed at the look on Raine's face. "Don't worry. He'll be nice. He's been just as worried about you as the rest of us. Maybe more," she added, leaving Raine to puzzle over her remark.

Martha bustled back into the room a few minutes later, a steaming bowl of soup in her hands. Raine's mouth watered as the nurse placed the bowl in front of her. "Mr. Duncan will be up shortly, so you eat. You can freshen up when you're done."

Raine nodded, her mouth full. After a second bowl, she felt almost as good as new. As she set the bowl aside, Charlotte breezed through the door.

"Raine! You look terrible!" The sincerity in Charlotte's voice was disturbing.

"Thanks. It's nice to see you too." Raine rolled her eyes, then gave her friend a gentle push. "Could you move, please? I want to get washed."

Martha shooed Charlotte out the door. "Plenty of time for you to talk to her later," she said with a smile. Martha turned to Raine. "Here's a washcloth and some soap. And a hairbrush and a mirror."

Raine washed her face. The warm water and fragrant soap had never felt so good. She picked up the hair brush and ran the brush through her hair, then froze as she realized how short it was. She picked up the mirror.

Was that really her? Her rich brown hair lay in waves, ending just below her chin. The looser style enhanced her high cheekbones and large eyes. Putting the mirror down, she stared at Martha.

"It'll grow back," the nurse promised.

Raine continued to stare, wide-eyed. "But why?"

"He had to do it, Raine. Otherwise you might not have escaped."

"He who? Who had to do it?"

"Good morning!"

Raine jumped at the sound of Mr. Duncan's voice.

"You're looking much better," he said.

She was taken aback by the kindness in his tone. H‹ seemed so—nice. Almost fatherly. . .

"How are you feeling, Raine?"

"Pretty fair," she said cautiously. He had never called h‹ Raine before, always Miss Thomas.

"Mr. Duncan, Martha said you could explain how I got her‹ to the Mission after, well, you know." She almost felt sick ‹ she thought of the dark, musty hold she had been forced t‹ live in for. . .for how long?

"Yes, well." He cleared his throat, sniffing nervously. "Ho‹ much do you remember?"

She wrinkled her brow. "I remember the man forcing m‹ from my room and into the carriage. I guess I fainted, becaus‹ when I came to, I was in the hold of some ship. I don't kno‹ how long I was there. My captor questioned me once. . ." H‹ voice trailed off as she pictured her captor's evil face.

She closed her eyes for a moment. "I don't remember muc‹ else, until a man came and found me. I thought it was Be‹ but it wasn't. The man was familiar, but I was so—" Sh‹ stopped short at the look on Mr. Duncan's face. "It was yo‹ wasn't it?"

He studied the floor.

She was incredulous. Never in a million years would sh‹ have guessed that the frosty Mission administrator woul‹ come to her rescue.

"How did you find me?" she asked in amazement.

"I was in my office the morning you were abducted, Raine‹ he said. "I heard some scuffling on the stairs, along with ‹ large thump on my door. At first I thought that some of th‹ children were being mischievous," he admitted. "I was jus‹ going to yank the door open when I heard a man swearin‹ Realizing there might be some sort of trouble, I waited until ‹ heard the front door open."

"But how did you. . ."

"I opened the door a crack, just in time to see him force yo‹ into the carriage." He clenched his teeth. "I slipped out th‹

back door and managed to get Oscar saddled in time to see the carriage turn the corner."

Raine stared at him in amazement. His eyes were glowing, his face animated.

"I followed the rascals to their ship and watched them manhandle you down to the hold. They had two guards posted, so I didn't even try to get aboard. I hated to leave you there, but I was going to need some help to rescue you. I went back to the Mission and I, well, I learned how to pray." His voice grew humble. "I've always been a pompous old thing, thinking that God was lucky to have me in His service. But when I realized how helpless I was to do anything about this situation, well, I just had to get down on my knees. Before I could even begin to pray for you, I knew I had to ask Christ for His forgiveness."

Mr. Duncan straightened in his chair. "Anyway, I gathered the staff together and we prayed. We kept watch on the ship day and night, trying to find a time when the guard would be the least likely to be alert. We were getting concerned about you being down there for so long, Raine, but they had someone posted constantly. Finally, we heard them talking excitedly about a big party planned for the next evening."

Mr. Duncan's gaze swept over her short hair and still-pale cheeks. "I didn't know what kind of condition I would find you in, Raine. It was pretty risky to try it in broad daylight, but in the end, I think it worked out fine."

She nodded, astounded at the risk that had been taken on her behalf.

Mr. Duncan's eyes traveled to her hair again. "We figured it would be less noticeable if you were not quite so, ah, so. . . noticeably a woman," he ended lamely, his face turning red. "Anyway, you're small enough that we hoped that everyone would think you were a young boy. I'm sorry I had to cut your hair." His eyes dropped to his hands. "So, I guess that's all. God was with us."

eight

Ben groaned as Violet captured yet another one of his pawns. "I just can't keep my mind on the game today, Violet," he apologized.

She eyed the young man sitting across from her. "I know it's hard, son, but surely you'll hear from Raine or her father soon."

"I hope so." He stared absently at the chess board, running his fingers through his hair. "It's just so hard not knowing what's going on!"

"The Lord has His hand on that gal, Ben. She'll be fine."

Later that evening, Ben sighed as he punched his pillow into a more comfortable shape. He had been in bed for hours, tossing and turning. *Christ, I know that I gave my life to You, and that I'm supposed to trust You. But I don't understand how You could let something bad happen to Raine. She loves You! I thought I was starting to get to know You, but I guess I don't. . .*

Unable to deal with his troubling thoughts, Ben got up and lit the lamp. Shivering, he grabbed his robe out of the massive wardrobe at the end of the bed. Being as quiet as possible, he eased the wardrobe door closed—and caught his toe on the leg of the bed as he turned. Losing his balance, he crashed into the wardrobe, sending an avalanche of boxes and bags crashing to the floor.

He sat up ruefully, certain that he had awakened Violet. He was silent for a long minute, listening, but he heard nothing except the faithful bonging of the grandfather clock. His shoulder ached from its meeting with the heavy oak door.

He stood, surveying the mess he had created. Feeling rather like a naughty little boy, he peered into one of boxes, laughing out loud as he pulled out a very fancy hat. Large and purple, it was covered with faded violets. Hastily putting the creation back in its box, he couldn't resist opening another box.

Another hat. This one was brown felt with a mink band. A matching mink muff lay in the bottom of the box. He carefully stacked the rest of the boxes, pushing them onto the top shelf of the wardrobe where it was apparent they had resided for quite some time. He brushed the dust off his hands, smiling as he imagined Violet wearing the wild purple hat. She must have been quite a fashionable lady in her day. He chuckled.

Closing the wardrobe firmly this time, he inched around the bed to avoid repeating the mishap. He glanced down as he heard the crunch of paper. Deciding that the yellowed paper must have fallen out of the wardrobe along with everything else, he stooped to pick it up.

He hadn't meant to read it, but as he glanced at the old letter, a sentence jumped out at him. His heart stopped. Sinking down on the side of the bed, he scanned the letter. Could it mean what he thought it did?

❧

Raine stood in front of her father's house, feeling her mouth grow dry.

"You can do it," Charlotte said.

Raine glanced at her friend. "I guess I'm just not sure I want to, Char." Grasping her bag, she marched to the big red door, wishing for Ben's comforting presence. It was nice to have Charlotte along, but it just wasn't the same.

She knocked. Hearing no movement from within, she knocked again with more energy. The house remained silent. She tried the doorknob, surprised as it turned easily in her hand.

Slipping through the door, she was gagged by the stale, closed-up odor of the house. *Surely Papa hasn't. . .* She couldn't bring herself to finish the thought. She set her bag down and tiptoed through the darkened living room, Charlotte close behind.

Reaching the hallway, she heard a faint sound coming from the bedroom. She felt like an intruder as she peeked around the corner. There. In the bed by the window. Her heart began to pound as she spotted him. "Papa!" She ran to him, taking his thin hand in hers. He moved restlessly, but didn't respond.

Raine was shocked at the gray in his hair, the dark hollows under his eyes. "Oh, Papa." She glanced around the room. Where was Dr. Delfin? She could tell someone had been here recently; her father's bed was neat and clean, a vase of fresh flowers was on the bedside table.

She settled herself in a chair next to her father, noticing that Charlotte had disappeared. She looked at the man lying in front of her. How he had changed! There were lines etched on his face that she had never seen before, lines of remorse and grief. She put her hand out, smoothing the graying hair off of his forehead. "I'm here, Papa," she whispered. "Please come back to me!" Exhausted, she let her head drop against the side of the bed.

She woke with a start as she sensed another's presence in the room. Recognizing Dr. Delfin, she sank back down in her chair. "I'm so glad you're here, Dr. Delfin. What's wrong with Papa?"

A smile lit the old doctor's face. "It's so good to see you, Raine," he said heartily. "We were concerned that something had happened to you."

"Yes, I was. . .delayed." Raine felt reluctant to add to his worries by telling of her abduction. "But how is Papa?"

She saw the shadows in the old doctor's eyes before he concealed them from her with a cheery smile. "I think you're going to be his best medicine, Raine."

"Doctor—"

"Ah, Raine. I can't lie to you. I can't help your father—he's dying of a broken heart. That's my best diagnosis."

Raine bowed her head. "If only he'd told us," she whispered.

"Then you know?" The old doctor sounded relieved. "You know that Paul was your half-brother?"

She nodded. "Paul evidently came across a copy of his birth certificate. He left it for me in a safety deposit box in Boston."

He sighed. "Miriam was so young. She had a terrible time delivering Paul. She hung on for a couple of hours, but I just couldn't save her." Dr. Delfin closed his eyes, reliving the painful day. "Your father was crushed. He had planned on marrying her, you know."

Raine shook her head. "No. All I knew was that the name listed on Paul's birth certificate wasn't the name of my mother. I didn't know any of the details."

"Paul's grandmother, his mother's mother, helped your father care for him for awhile. Then Richard met Ellen. She was willing to take Paul as her own."

Raine was silent, pondering the strength her mother must have had.

"It was a happy day when they added you to their family, Raine."

She smiled absently, her thoughts perplexed. "But why. . . why did they keep it all such a secret?"

Dr. Delfin shrugged. "It's not easy to admit failures, Raine. Especially to your children. And when he became a clergyman, your father felt even more pressure to keep his past sins a secret."

"But for Papa to accuse Paul of doing the same thing he had done. . ." Raine's sentence trailed off as she thought of her brother. What added pain it must have been to discover his father's sin, hidden all these years.

The doctor nodded, his face grave. "It was your father's own guilt that made him so furious with your brother. But he only made his guilt worse when he sent Paul away. All these years, for all that he's a man of God, he's let guilt eat at him, consuming him. I suspect he became a clergyman as a way to try to atone for his sins—but of course we can never create our own atonement. God's forgiveness is the only medicine that can cure him now."

❧

John waved the paper wildly in front of Ben's nose. "Praise God! She's safe!"

Ben snatched the telegram from his hand. Reading the brief message, he let out a huge sigh of relief. "Thank God," he murmured, longing to hold her in his arms, to reassure himself that she really was fine.

"It says she'll be writing soon to tell us everything. I can't wait to hear what happened." Noticing Ben's silence, John put a hand on the younger man's shoulder. "What is it, Ben?"

Ben stared at John, misery filling his eyes. "I doubted God," he whispered, dropping his gaze. "I questioned Him. I was angry that He would allow something to happen to Raine."

John's eyes softened. "Ah, Ben," he sighed. "Everyone has questioned God at one time or another. We're human, and humans are weak sometimes. But He still loves you. Just because you failed doesn't mean it's all over."

Ben looked up hopefully as John smiled. "Just ask Him to forgive you, son. Then ask Him to help you do better next time. You're going to be just fine, Captain," John continued, "especially when that pretty little niece of mine gets back!" He chuckled at the look on Ben's face.

"I love her, John," Ben said seriously.

"I know you do, son. I know."

ঽঽ

Raine tossed and turned on her makeshift bed. She strained to hear her father's breathing. Convinced he was resting comfortably, she lay back down on the cot she had set up next to his bed.

Morning dawned at last, and she felt his eyes on her face before she was even fully awake. "Good morning, Papa," she said softly.

He started. "I thought I was imagining things!" Slow tears trickled out of his eyes as she rushed to his side. "I thought I would never see you again in this world, Raine."

She smoothed his hair back with gentle fingers. "I'm here now, Papa," she assured him. "I'll take care of you." She longed to ask him about Paul, but that would have to wait until he was stronger. He closed his eyes then, a faint smile on his lips, and she sat by his bedside until he fell asleep.

Studying him, she was amazed at the changes that had overtaken him since the last time she had been home. Richard

Thomas was just a shell of the handsome, robust man he had once been. Pondering this, she felt the last shreds of bitterness toward her father dissolve. Sorrow took its place, sorrow that a once-strong man of God had allowed himself to slip into so much sin and pain.

Why, Papa? she cried silently for the hundredth time. *We loved you. You didn't have to deceive us. We wouldn't have forsaken you even if we had known the truth.*

Dr. Delfin stopped by in the evening, thrilled to find his patient resting quietly. "Ah, I knew you would be the best medicine in the world, Raine. Now, if we could only find that brother of yours."

Oh, no. "Papa doesn't know where Paul is?"

Dr. Delfin looked surprised. "Not to my knowledge. Do you know where he is?"

She shook her head, disappointment flooding through her. "I thought, well, I assumed that. . ."

"Your father lost contact with Paul just after he learned that Paul survived the shipwreck."

Raine frowned. "He knows as much as I do, then," she said, sighing. "I thought for sure Papa could tell me where Paul was."

Had she come this far only to be stymied again? She felt hot tears begin to gather, and she saw Charlotte and the doctor exchange glances over her head.

"Come on, Raine," Charlotte said. "Let's get a breath of fresh air."

She nodded, following Charlotte out the door. It did feel good to be out in the warm sunshine after being in Papa's dark little room for so long. She took several deep breaths of pine-scented air and swallowed the lump in her throat. "I don't know what's wrong with me, Char." She bent to pick a sprig of lily-of-the-valley. "I should be happy that Papa's doing some better, and I am, but I was just so sure that he would tell me where Paul was."

"God's timing is perfect, Raine."

Raine lifted the tiny flowers to her nose, breathing in the

delicate perfume. Charlotte was right, of course. She should be used to unfamiliar paths by now. "Don't stop praying for me, friend."

Charlotte smiled. "Never. Now, let's go get something to eat. I know how grumpy you get when you're hungry."

"I can't help it that I've been blessed with a healthy appetite, can I?"

Charlotte rolled her eyes. "Healthy? Try hearty. Or hoggish. Or manly. Or. . ."

Raine laughed, in spite of her worry. "All right, all right. Lead the way to the pig trough."

✿

But disappointment still lay heavily on her that night as she tried to sleep. Her father had only awakened for brief periods throughout the evening, so she had no opportunity to question him about Paul. *Where are you, Paul? I thought I was so close.*

She pulled the covers up more snugly around her neck. *Father, I know You've led me thus far. Thank You for delivering me from my captor, and thank You for keeping Papa until I could see him one more time. Please continue to guide me to Paul.* Finally drifting to sleep, she dreamed sweet dreams of Ben. Waking in the morning, he filled her thoughts. If only he weren't so far away!

"Raine?" She jumped as she heard her father's weak voice.

"Coming, Papa!" She hurriedly brushed her hair, smoothing it back as she entered her father's room. "How are you this morning, Papa?"

"I was hoping I hadn't dreamed that you were here."

"I'm really here, Papa," she assured him again. "I came as soon as I got the telegram from Dr. Delfin, but I was delayed in London for a few days." Giving him no time to question her, she quickly asked, "Are you ready for breakfast this morning?"

Her father raised an eyebrow. "Did Dr. Delfin appoint you as my personal nurse?" he teased, showing the first hint of his old self that Raine had seen since she arrived.

"Yes, he did, as a matter of fact." She smiled at him. "So— will it be oatmeal or toast?"

After he had eaten, her father put his napkin down with a tired smile. "Thank you, Raine. That was delicious."

"Are you ready to rest, Papa? Here, I'll help you. . ."

He pushed her hand away. "I'm tired of resting."

She sat back on her heels, waiting as he shifted restlessly, avoiding her gaze.

"I think we need to talk, Raine," he said at last.

Her heart began to pound. Now that the time had come, she wasn't sure she could handle hearing everything. "Papa—"

"I need to do this, Raine." Her father looked her in the eye. "I need to make things right." Averting his eyes again, he stared at the wall. "I just don't know where to begin."

Raine put a gentle hand on his. "I love you, Papa," she said quietly. "No matter what you have to tell me, I love you."

Richard Thomas heaved, and then sobs forced themselves out of his mouth in great gasps. It was long moments before he could speak. "You don't know what I've done, Raine. I've been so miserable." Tears poured down his face. "I forced my own son away, condemning him for something he didn't do. In my heart I knew all along he didn't do it—and then when that girl finally admitted publicly that the father of her baby was someone else. I was wrong. . .so wrong. . ."

She let him cry, knowing that he had to deal with it in his own way. Richard finally pulled himself together. Reaching for his daughter's hand, he held on tightly as if to gain strength from her. "I accused Paul of the very thing I was guilty of," he whispered in agony. "I don't know how to tell you this, Raine, but. . ."

"I know, Papa."

"What?"

"I already know." She explained how Paul had left his birth certificate in the safety deposit box. "Dr. Delfin filled in the details for me, Papa. You don't have to talk about it any more."

Her father hung his head. "I thought you and Paul would never have to know, that it would somehow be easier that way. But I've never forgiven myself. I should have. . ."

"Papa—"

"There's more, Raine." Richard looked at his daughter intently now, seemingly determined to get everything out in the open. "I'm sure you've agonized over not hearing from your brother all this time. He wrote you many letters, Raine."

She gasped. "Then why. . .?"

He closed his eyes in pain. "I was being eaten alive by guilt, Raine. When it appeared that Paul had committed the same sin that I had been hiding, it just compounded my own guilt and pain. I felt that I had been a failure as a father; that somehow my sin had been passed down to my son even without his knowledge. I'm afraid I took out all those frustrations on Paul."

"But—the letters?"

"I was so angry, Raine. I didn't want to ever see Paul again. Just the sight of him enflamed my guilt. I didn't even want you to have anything to do with him, so I read the letters myself—something inside me still cared enough about him to want to know where he was and how he was doing. But then I burned every letter." He buried his face in his hands. "You'll never know how sorry I am," he groaned.

"Oh, Papa." *No wonder Paul thought I had turned my back on him,* Raine mourned.

Her father took a deep breath. "I still loved your brother deeply, even though I was furious with him. I couldn't bring myself to speak his name out loud—but I had to know if he was safe, if he was telling the truth in his letters to you. I. . .I had him followed."

Raine stared at her father, feeling befuddled. What was he saying?

He sighed. "I hired a man to trail Paul, Raine. He reported back to me Paul's whereabouts and so on."

"Then why don't you know where he is now?" She winced as she heard the sharpness in her own voice.

Her father shook his head, infinite weariness in his eyes. "I don't know, Raine. My man had reported to me that Paul was recovering well from his injuries after the shipwreck. Then apparently without warning, Paul left in the middle of the night. Langley hasn't been able to track him down."

The words echoed in Raine's mind, triggering an avalanche of questions. "Papa, do you think Paul knew he was being followed?"

Richard frowned. "I don't think. . .why?"

She described the message Paul had sent her in the locket. " 'Am being pursued' was the first sentence," she explained. "He also mentioned something about that in the letter," she remembered thoughtfully. "Do you think. . .?"

Her father was still frowning. "I don't think so, Raine," he said slowly. "I'm sure he could have noticed Langley following him, but I don't think he would have been perceived as a threat." Richard pictured the scrawny little man he had chosen to trail Paul. "No, I don't think so."

The evil face of a red-haired man popped into Raine's mind. Suddenly, she knew who had been pursuing her brother, and it wasn't Langley. "I think you need to rest now, Papa," she said firmly. "I forgive you for everything you did—and I know the Lord will as soon as you ask Him. Why don't you just talk to Jesus for a little while, and then go to sleep. We'll talk more later."

Her father closed his eyes without a word, and Raine breathed a sigh of relief as she stepped out of the stuffy room. Her head ached with the events of the day, and her heart was heavy with thoughts of Paul. The thought of her brother being hunted by the man who had been her captor sent chills down her spine.

"So how's Papa doing?" Charlotte's voice interrupted her thoughts.

Raine smiled. "Much better, now that he has started to deal with the past. I think we'll leave tomorrow. Now that Papa has turned back to the Lord, he's as anxious for me to find Paul as I am." She looked thoughtful, then added, "But before we go, there is an item of business we need to take care of."

"We?"

"Yes, we. I need you for moral support. We need to do a bit of sleuthing, that's all."

"This is where Geoff and Christina's house stood before it burned," Raine whispered to Charlotte.

"So now where do we go?" Charlotte whispered back.

Raine shrugged. "Let's look around a little. It doesn't look like anyone even takes care of the place anymore."

It felt eerie to walk through the deserted grounds. How well she could remember all the fun they had had here. It wasn't that long ago, really, that she and Christina climbed these old apple trees to spy on their brothers, giggling wildly when they were caught. . .

"Raine, I think we need to go." Charlotte's loud whisper held a note of panic. "There's someone. . ."

Raine jumped as a man appeared as if from nowhere. Turning to flee, the sound of his voice froze her.

"Raine! Please. It's just me."

She turned slowly to meet the plea in his blue eyes. "Geoff?"

He nodded.

"You've been following me."

He nodded again.

"Why?" Her heartbeat was returning to normal.

"Because I wanted. . .needed to make things right." His disfigured face twisted into an odd sort of grimace. "I couldn't find Paul."

Out of the corner of her eye, Raine noticed Charlotte peeking out from behind the outhouse. "It seems that no one can find Paul, Geoff. But how. . . I mean, I thought. . .?"

"You thought that I was dead."

She nodded.

"I thought I was dead, too. It was horrible." He passed a trembling hand over his eyes. "I'll spare you the details, but suffice it to say that the road to recovery was very, very long. But there is good that has come of it." She looked into his glowing eyes. "I have come to know Jesus Christ, Raine. I mean, really know Him."

She watched as the tears coursed down his face, feeling her heart respond to the intensity of his feelings. "I hurt Paul so badly," he choked. He turned away, trying to compose himself. "And I know that must have hurt you as well. Can you forgive me, Raine?"

She nodded, though she wasn't sure what she was forgiving.

Geoff fell silent for a long moment. "I need to confess something," he said finally.

Raine looked at him, her eyebrows raised, but Geoff could no longer meet her eyes. "It was me," he said in a low voice. "It was me that made all the trouble for Paul."

Raine shook her head, confused. "You didn't make the trouble, Geoff. It was Lucinda who told that lie—and of course you weren't the baby's real father. What are you talking about?"

Geoff hesitated, then took a deep breath. "I was angry with Paul, jealous I guess. We'd always been so close, doing everything together, and then suddenly he seemed to have outgrown me. And I hated him for hurting Christina. I was so angry that when a man came to the house with a coded message Paul had written me, I said I didn't know anything about it. I told the man that Paul had stolen that old code book from me—though really he'd only borrowed it—and I said that I had no idea what he wanted it for. I told him that Paul had been acting very strangely. I didn't mean anything by it, I had no idea the sort of mess I was getting Paul into. I just was angry at him. I was pretty sure the man was some sort of policeman and I thought it would serve Paul right to get in a little trouble. I never dreamt. . ."

He fell silent again. Raine stared at him, stunned by what he had told her. "I never knew. . ."

He nodded. "No one knew. Except for me. Pretty soon another man came to the house, asking about Paul. He showed me a message in code, but it wasn't written in Paul's handwriting. He asked me if I'd ever seen anything like it before. I wasn't really paying attention, I was impatient to be on my way to the hunt at the Presteigns', and without thinking, I said, yes, I've seen lots of messages like that. The man looked angry and asked me where I'd seen them. I said Paul had given them to me, which was the truth of course, because he was always writing messages to me in code. The man asked where the messages were now. I had my horse saddled by then, and I just laughed and told him they were all back in my room. I swung up on the horse and rode past him." Geoff shuddered. "That night our house burned and I—" He touched his face. "Nothing was ever the same."

Raine could not speak. Finally, her voice trembling, she asked, "Why did everyone say you had died?"

Geoff shrugged. "I asked my family to spread the story I was dead. I'd been thinking about that man, the red-haired one I'd spoken to the day before our house burned. I knew he was no policeman, and I understood now that he thought I knew something about coded messages. I was afraid he'd come back."

Raine's face was very white. "Red-haired?"

Geoff nodded. "He had red hair. And a tattoo on his hand. I think he must have been a sailor."

❧

Raine waved until Mr. Duncan, Charlotte, and the Mission staff were mere specks on the wharf. She felt ridiculous dressed up like an elderly woman, but everyone had insisted on it for her safety. "You never know, Raine," Mr. Duncan had said. "Ol' Red Hair didn't seem like the type to give up easily."

In the end, Raine had given in to their pleas to travel incognito. Now at last she was on board and headed back to Ben. Leaving Papa had been hard, but he had encouraged her to go.

"Find my boy, Raine," he had pled. "I need to make things right before I go to meet the Father."

"I'll find Paul if it takes the rest of my life, Papa," she pledged solemnly. She squeezed his hand. "Pray for me."

Tears glistened in the old man's eyes. "I will, Raine. I will."

She smiled as she gazed out across the waters of the Atlantic. She thought fondly of her father, thankful that they had had the chance to cry together and pray together. *It's like we have a whole new relationship,* she thought gratefully. *Now, if I could only find Paul.*

God was at work. Hadn't Mr. Duncan recommitted his life to the Lord because of that situation? And then there was the telegram she had received from Ben, telling of his surrender to

Christ. It would be wonderful to be in his arms again, this time to share his new-found joy.

She had decided to surprise him, so she had not wired her plans to return to Boston. Her heart beat faster as she imagined their reunion. Of course, if he saw her like this. . . She giggled, fluffing her gray hair. "You look just like my great-aunt Esther," Charlotte had said, barely suppressing her giggles as Raine had adjusted the frumpy hat to a more rakish angle.

So much had happened since that day she had waved good-bye to Ben in Boston. She couldn't wait to share the glad news about her father and hoped that Ben had some good news of his own about Paul. *And Aunt Grace will be so relieved that Papa is doing better,* she thought.

The salty spray misted her face, reminding her of all the times she and Ben had stood at the railing on the *Capernaum* . . .their first tender words. . .their shared hopes and dreams. . .

૨

Near Santa Fe, New Mexico

It was time. Tom had awakened before dawn with a sense of urgency pounding in his breast. It was time to go home.

He roused the sleepy cowhands, prodding them into action while it was still dark. "What's the rush, boss?" Simon drawled.

Tom shrugged. "It's time."

It's time, it's time. . .the phrase seemed to keep beat with Trixie's galloping hooves. The sense of expectancy that Tom had come to know like his shadow crescendoed with every passing mile.

nine

Ben sat at a corner table in yet another tavern, trying to keep the disgust from showing on his face. Now that he knew Raine was safe, he was concentrating on finding Paul. Raine had told him about her aunt thinking she had seen Paul outside a tavern, and Ben had decided the taverns would be a good place to try and get some information on where Paul had gone. He brushed a fly from his face with a grimace. He never had been able to figure out what the attraction was to these hot, stuffy places. The women were coarse and loud, the atmosphere thick with smoke and schemes. But surely if Paul had been here someone would remember him.

After questioning the people in the tavern, though, he was no closer to finding Paul. He stood blinking in the sunlight, filling his lungs with fresh air. *I just can't go to another one of these places today,* he decided. *One more day won't matter.* Turning to untie the horses, his heart sank as he met the icy gaze of Raine's aunt Grace. She leaned out of her carriage, staring at him in horror as he left the tavern, but before he could call to her, her carriage moved forward with a lurch and rattled away from him.

He pulled his horses to a stop in front of Violet's house, hardly realizing what he was doing, stunned that Raine's aunt would think the worst of him, without giving him a chance to explain. He had to admit that it looked bad for him to be coming out of a tavern, especially since he had recently committed his life to the Lord. *But I didn't do anything wrong,* his heart protested.

Slumping despondently on the edge of the bed, he pondered the situation. *What should I do next? God, please lead me to the right place. I know someone has to remember Paul. I just know it.*

The next morning found him in the sea front district, standing in front of the Red Witch Tavern. Taking a deep breath of the salty air, he heaved the door open. Waiting a moment for his eyes to adjust, he took in the heavy smell of ale and the high-pitched laughter of the women. How he hated this! He ran his fingers through his hair as he leaned back in his chair, catching the eye of the blonde-haired girl behind the counter.

She grabbed a glass off the shelf behind her with a practiced motion and hurried over to him. He placed his order for a glass of lemonade and she returned with it promptly. Ben nodded his gratitude, then spoke to her softly, asking her the same question he had asked all the others.

She froze. "Paul?" she whispered, her face white. "Yes, I know Paul."

Ben looked at her trembling lips and wide eyes. "Can we talk outside?" he asked, glancing around at the growing audience.

He opened the door for her, following as she walked stiffly outside.

"Are you all right, Miss. . .?"

"Hathaway. Christina Hathaway," she supplied. "I'm fine. It's just that. . . I just. . ." She looked up at Ben, her heart in her eyes. "Do you know where Paul is?"

Christina. He remembered something Raine had told him about her childhood friends and understanding glimmered. "No, I don't know where Paul is, Christina," he said regretfully. "I was hoping you could help me find him." He introduced himself, giving her a thumbnail sketch of what he knew of Paul.

"Well, I saw him after the *Aramathea* went down," she said. "He came here to. . .to have a drink."

He came here to say good-bye, Ben surmised. "Did he say anything about where he was going?"

She considered the question. "Not really, I guess," she admitted. "But he always talked about a life-long dream that he had." She smiled wistfully. "He was going to take me with him."

🍂

Raine stood on deck, her heart pounding as the familiar sight of the Boston harbor came into view. She could almost feel Ben's arms around her. . .

One of the first passengers to disembark, she waited impatiently, flagging down the first driver she saw. She gave him the address of her uncle's house and settled back in the seat. Glancing about as the carriage pulled away from the waterfront, her heart stopped as she caught a glimpse of a tall, blond man. Ben! She craned her neck, trying to get a closer look. His back was to Raine, but she could see that he was in earnest conversation with a young woman. It sure looked like Ben, but why would he be standing in front of a tavern, talking to someone who looked like she belonged behind the counter pouring drinks?

Raine decided her longing for him was causing her imagination to run away with her. Dismissing the incident, she decided to freshen up a bit. She powdered her nose and patted her short locks into place, smiling as she imagined her aunt's shocked reaction. True, her hair had grown out some, but the rich brown waves still hung well above her shoulders. At least she had discarded the gray wig and baggy clothes after a few days at sea.

She giggled, picturing her family's reaction if she had decided to come home masquerading as an elderly woman. As it was, they might still look at her askance. She shrugged, gathering her things quickly as they neared the house.

Aunt Grace reacted to Raine's new hairstyle better than she had expected, and she barely had time to dash a short note off to Ben before she was pressed into telling of her adventures in London.

Her aunt and uncle were horrified as she told of her abduction. Aunt Grace clucked over her like a mother hen. Uncle John sat silently, at last breathing a quiet "Praise God!" when she had finished bringing them up to date.

Raine sighed as her story drew to a close. "I had so hoped that Papa knew where he was, but. . .maybe Ben found something more," she said hopefully. "I sent him a note to let him know I'm back. Maybe he'll come tonight."

Grace looked uncomfortable. "Raine, I hate to give you bad news. . ."

"Now, Grace," John spoke sternly. "Let the young people work things out for themselves."

Raine looked from one to the other. "What is this all about?"

"Don't you worry about it, Raine. You just go on upstairs and freshen yourself. I'm sure Captain Ben will be coming as soon as he receives your note." John stared hard at his wife.

Upstairs, Raine closed the door to her room and sank down on the bed, relieved that her journey was over. It felt good to have a steady floor beneath her feet. She pondered what to wear when Ben saw her for the first time.

Shaking the folds out of her favorite navy blue dress, she hung it up in the spacious wardrobe. *Maybe I ought to wear the green one. . .* Her thoughts were interrupted by a knock at the door.

She opened the door to her aunt. "Which one do you like best?" she asked, indicating the two dresses.

Her aunt closed the door behind her silently, ignoring the question. She wore an agitated look on her face. "Raine," she whispered. "Your uncle would be very angry if he knew I was up here, but I feel I have to tell you."

Raine frowned as Grace bit her lip. "I don't know how to tell you this, Raine." Her eyes filled with tears. "I was at the dressmaker's shop the other day, you know, on Grape Street."

Raine nodded, wondering what could possibly be so upsetting to her aunt.

"Anyway, I decided to drive down the street to Eva's Bakery to get some of that wonderful rye bread she makes." Raine nodded again, her curiosity growing. "I was almost to Eva's, when I glanced across the street, and I saw Ben come out of a tavern!"

Raine's mind instantly flashed to the man she had seen standing outside the Red Witch Tavern. Surely there must be a reason. . .

"Are you sure it was Ben?"

Her aunt nodded. "I'm sorry, Raine."

"I'd like to be alone, please, Auntie," Raine said softly.

"Of course, dear. I'm so sorry."

Raine eased down onto the bed, her mind reeling. Could that have been Ben who was talking to the tavern girl at the wharf? The more she thought of it, the more sure she became that it had to have been him. She pictured again the way the man had leaned eagerly toward the fancily dressed woman, and her heart froze.

Picturing his face, his tender blue eyes, she just couldn't believe that he would betray her trust. *I'm sure he'll explain the situation to me,* she told herself firmly. *He loves me.*

Pushing aside the nagging doubts, she finally settled on the mint green dress. Brushing her short hair, she wondered what Ben's reaction would be when he saw her. She dabbed on some of her favorite lilac perfume.

By nine o'clock, Raine conceded to the fact that Ben wasn't coming. She thought she had heard someone at the door earlier, but decided she must have been mistaken since no one had called her. Still unwilling to believe the worst of the man she loved, she told herself that he must have had something come up that prevented him from coming to her.

She undressed slowly, laying her dress over the chair. Crawling into bed, she lay staring at the ceiling, feeling more exhausted than she ever had in her life. Her anticipation of seeing Ben and the ensuing disappointment had drained her. "I know you'll come to me tomorrow, my love," she murmured as sleep claimed her.

❧

Ben threw the rest of his luggage into the carriage, closing the door with a grim smile. Stooping down, he placed a kiss on the forehead of the elderly woman in the wheelchair. "Pray for me, Violet," he requested softly.

She nodded, a single tear escaping to run down her wrinkled cheek. "God go with you, Ben," she whispered. "Tell Paul I love him."

Ben stared straight ahead as the train chugged steadily westward. The ache in his heart throbbed louder than the train's engine, and the lonely whistle echoed his feelings. He still couldn't believe that Raine had refused to see him. He had assumed that her aunt would tell her about the tavern incident, but he had fully expected Raine to give him a chance to explain. *I love her, God,* he groaned inwardly. *I thought she loved me, too. Why didn't she trust me enough to let me explain?* Closing his eyes, he was finally lulled to sleep by the clacking of the rails; the pain in his heart dulled by slumber.

❧

"Raine!" The pounding on her door dragged her from a dreamless sleep. She jumped out of bed and grabbed her robe just as her uncle burst into the room.

"Hurry up, Raine!" John was frantic. "Get dressed! We've got to catch Ben before he leaves!"

Raine stared at her uncle, unmoving. He thrust her dress at her. "Hurry! I'll explain on the way." He turned, closing the door behind him.

Catch Ben before he leaves? She had no time to think before her uncle was pounding on her door again. "Raine! Let's go!"

She jerked open the door and flew down the stairs behind her uncle. He fairly pushed her into the carriage, slapping the startled horses with the reins. "We'll be there in a minute, Raine."

Jerking to a stop in front of the train station, he jumped out of the carriage. "Wait here. I'll be right back!" He tore across the crowded lobby, pushing his way to the front of the long ticket line.

She stared after him, dumbfounded, then watched her uncle heading back to the carriage, his shoulders slumping. "We're too late, Raine. I'm sorry."

"What are we too late for, Uncle John?"

"Don't be angry with your aunt, Raine. She did what she thought was best for you, but she's often a short-sighted woman." He sighed. "Ben came to see you last night, Raine.

Your aunt told him you didn't want to see him."

"Oh no!" Raine cried. "Why? How could she?"

"I didn't find out about it until this morning. I drove over to Violet's house as soon as I realized what had happened, but she said he had already left for the train station."

"Left?" Raine's voice was strangled.

Her uncle nodded. "Violet said he had gotten some information on Paul, and he decided to follow the lead."

"Where? Where did he go?" Her heart felt like lead.

"I think you'll have to talk to Violet," John replied.

৵

At Violet's house, Raine shook her head in disbelief. "I can't believe what you're telling me, Violet."

"It's true, honey. I really am Paul's grandmother. I hadn't planned on telling anyone, but when John recognized me and Ben found that letter, I decided that it wasn't really all that secret anymore."

"But, how. . .?"

Violet smiled. "God must have brought Paul to me, Raine. I had started taking in boarders, and then one day, Paul showed up, asking for a room. He had been asking around for a place to stay, and someone had told him my name. By that time he had seen the birth certificate and had guessed the truth about the circumstances surrounding his birth. When he heard my last name, he recognized that it was the same as his mother's, and so he came to me, asking for a place to board." She sighed and her eyes grew misty. "I hadn't seen him since he was three years old, and even though he favors his father, he still carries a distinct resemblance to his mother. My dear, sweet Miriam."

Raine swallowed hard.

"Paul was afraid to ask and I didn't tell him who I was right away." Violet wiped at her eyes. "He was so precious to me! We came to be friends, and after awhile I told him what he had already suspected."

"But why did he leave Boston, Violet?"

Violet's face was troubled. "I don't know, Raine. I've asked myself that a million times." She shook her head. "He just seemed like a different person after the ship sank."

"Different?"

"Yes, he seemed. . .skittish. He had some pretty nasty wounds, and at first I attributed his nervousness to the trauma of the shipwreck. But I don't know. It was almost as if he were expecting something bad to happen." Violet lowered her eyes. "I had saved up some money over the years, hoping to give it to Paul someday. He is my only grandchild, you know. I gave it to him after he came back from the *Aramathea* that last time."

Raine was touched by the love she saw in Violet's eyes. "I'm sure Paul was very grateful," she said softly. "But how does Ben fit into the picture?"

"Ben found a letter one night in Paul's old room. The letter was addressed to me, written by my daughter while she was still pregnant with Paul. Ben realized right away what it meant and confronted me with it." She smiled. "He was sure I knew where Paul was and that I was keeping it a secret from everyone."

Raine could see Ben in her mind's eye, trying to coax Violet to tell him where Paul was.

"But then where did Ben go if he didn't know where to look? He couldn't have just made a wild guess." Raine was puzzled.

"Oh, my, no!" Violet was astonished. "He talked to someone who knew Paul. She gave him a couple places to start looking. Didn't you know that?"

She? Raine shook her head. *How could this have turned into such a mess?*

". . .in Colorado Springs," Violet was saying.

"What?"

"I said, the young woman told Ben that she thought Paul might have gone to Colorado."

"Colorado!" In all her imaginings about Paul, she had never envisioned him going west. "Why in the world. . .so did Ben go to Colorado?"

Violet nodded. "That he did, Raine. He was looking pretty broken-hearted when he left. If I were you, I would get myself out there, too. I have a feeling that there are two men there who would give a pretty penny to see your face."

❧

Ben stepped off the train, breathing in the cool mountain air. Exiting the Denver and Rio Grande depot, he gazed appreciatively at the welcoming city of Colorado Springs. Taking in another deep breath of the tangy, pine-scented air, he felt as if he were awakening from a long sleep. The pain that had weighted his heart and deadened his senses for days lifted slightly, allowing him a fresh view on life.

He checked into the Copper Mine Inn, then quickly returned to the outdoors, reveling in the brilliant blue sky and beautiful snow-capped mountains.

The sense of welcome that he had felt initially deepened until it almost felt like a homecoming. Shuffling his feet in the golden autumn leaves, he lifted his hat to feel the warmth of the sun on his head. *Thank You, Father,* he breathed.

❧

The crisp autumn days slid swiftly by. Ben had inquired in all the businesses up and down Pikes Peak Avenue, even questioning some of the street car drivers. Nothing.

He made forays to the outlying ranches. Still nothing. Could Christina have been mistaken? Or was Paul refusing to be found? Grasping at straws, he secured a pack mule and spent several days combing the area as far as Cripple Creek. He was awed by the masses of golden-leafed aspens fluttering in the fall breeze and the hidden valleys filled with wildflowers. The Rocky Mountains themselves were beautiful beyond words, filled with crags, meadows, and canyons. But the search for Paul was at another dead end.

Ben had used every resource at his disposal, including an advertisement in the *Colorado Springs Gazette*. Even an afternoon spent poring over the records at the El Paso County courthouse turned up nothing but disappointment. He should just pack up and go back to London; at least he could do what Paul had asked him to do in his letter. But he wanted to see Paul first, make sure he was really the man Ben thought he was. He couldn't give up. Not yet.

He prayed continually for wisdom and guidance, gradually feeling the now-familiar peace of God surround him. Though his heart still ached for Raine, he had begun to sense that God had brought him here for a specific purpose. Lying in bed at night, he would feel the undeniable tug on his heart.

He had grown uncomfortable with the thought of running the shipping business for the rest of his life. *But that's all I know how to do,* he reminded himself. *Well, except for. . .* He sat up abruptly. *Surely not! Surely You aren't calling me to be a. . .a pastor!* He could hardly think it. He lay back down slowly, his thoughts racing. *But I haven't known You for very long. Surely I'm not ready to. . .to lead others?*

It was true that there seemed to be a dearth of churches in the outlying areas. Where did the ranchers and country folk go to church? He would wager that they would feel too uncomfortable to attend the imposing churches he had noticed in town. *But why choose me, God? I don't know if I could do it.*

In all thy ways acknowledge Him, and He shall direct thy paths. The Scripture rang in his mind with such clarity that he knew it would change his life forever.

❧

He awoke the next morning, a sense of wonder filling his heart. "Please lead me, Father," he prayed earnestly. "And please minister to Raine. I love her so, Father. I don't want to be without her for the rest of my life. Please bring her back to me!"

He sat in the hotel dining room, absently chewing his apple pie. He couldn't believe he was actually considering the possibility of staying in Colorado Springs, yet he could not deny the tugging at his heart that grew stronger day by day. *I'd have to go to London to sell my share of the business,* he mused. *While I'm there I'll see those papers of Paul's get into the right hands.* He grinned in spite of himself. *Father will never believe that I'm finally going to quit sailing.* He chuckled out loud, then sobered. *Am I? Am I willing to sell a thriving business to become a cowboy preacher?*

ten

"God go with you!" The farewells of Raine's aunt and uncle rang in her ears. Settling herself into a seat by the window, she craned her neck. Yes, they were still there, waving furiously as the train huffed away from the station.

She waved back until the train rounded the first bend. Sitting back with a sigh, she closed her eyes, glad for the first real moment of quiet she had had in quite a while. It seemed like she had done nothing but rush, rush, rush since Ben left two weeks ago. But now she was finally headed westward.

West! Never in a million years had she thought that her search for Paul would lead her to a place like Colorado. She pictured herself arriving at the depot in Colorado Springs to find it surrounded by Indians. Or maybe the cowboys made sure the Indians stayed in the mountains.

She shivered. What kind of place was she going to? Surely there would be some place for her to stay. She remembered the photographs of log cabins she had seen once. *I don't know if I'm ready for this,* she thought. But maybe Ben had already found Paul, and she wouldn't have to stay in that wild country at all. Not that she was scared, exactly. Just a bit anxious.

It's only for a little while, she told herself. Yet somehow, she had a feeling deep within her heart that it would be a long, long time before she saw Boston again. Aunt Grace evidently had the same feeling.

"It's all my fault," Grace had sobbed. "If I hadn't sent Ben away, you wouldn't be running off all alone to that forsaken place." She blew her nose loudly. "How are you even going to find Ben once you get there?"

"Now Gracie, God works in mysterious ways. If God is sending Raine to Colorado, He'll take care of her."

Good old Uncle John. Raine smiled fondly as she recalled

his parting comment to her.

"You just trust the Lord, Raine. I've got a feeling He has something amazing waiting for you."

"I do too, Uncle John. I do too," she murmured now, watching the miles roll by. *What is it, Father?* she questioned silently.

Squirming around in an attempt to find a more comfortable position, her eye fell on the small package Christina had thrust into her hand just before she left. Following a hunch, Raine had taken a jaunt down to the waterfront the day before she was to leave for Colorado. Then it was just a matter of waiting before Christina slipped out of the door of the Red Witch tavern.

"So you're the woman I saw Ben talking to," Raine exclaimed after she and Christina had hugged each other.

Christina nodded. "God must have led him to me. Although he said he'd been searching in all the taverns, asking if anyone knew anything about Paul."

"And you were able to tell Ben where Paul is now?"

Christina's eyes clouded. "I haven't heard from Paul for over three years now. But he always dreamed of going west, to Colorado."

"And that's where I'm headed now." Raine shook her head. "I can't believe I have to go now, when I've just found you, Christina."

Her old friend nodded. "I know. It's so good to see you. I'd love for us to spend some time together."

"Why don't you go to Colorado with me? You could find a nice place to work out there. Maybe be a seamstress or something."

Despair filled Christina's eyes. "I would give anything to go, Raine. But I'm bound for three more months."

"Well, maybe we'll all be back by then. Christy—" Raine stopped. She looked at Christina thoughtfully, afraid to ask the question that hovered on her lips.

"You're wondering why Paul didn't take me with him." Christina sighed. "It's a long story, Raine, but suffice it to say

that he did it to protect me."

Raine raised her eyebrows.

"I think Paul will have to be the one to explain it to you, Raine. I don't think I even know the whole story."

She could see that Christina had said all she was going to say. "You love him."

"Yes. I always have. You know that."

Raine nodded.

"Find him for me, Ray. He needs me."

Raine felt her throat get tight. "I'll do my best, Christy. Pray for me."

"Always." Christina bit her lip. "Would you give this to him when you find him?"

Raine reached out for the small package, asking no questions.

❧

By the third day of her journey, Raine's anticipation had grown to a feverish pitch. How close was she to finding Paul? Maybe Ben had already found him, and they would both be waiting for her at the depot. No, that was silly. Neither of them even knew she was coming. Then too, maybe Ben was still upset with her. She couldn't wait to set everything straight again. She pictured their reunion, her stomach fluttering at the thought of it. She finally took to getting off the train at every stop, pacing around the boarding area to relieve some of her pent-up energy.

She lay in her berth that night, lulled into drowsiness by the steady clacking of the train wheels. Tomorrow, tomorrow, tomorrow, they seemed to sing. Tomorrow—what would she find? She felt as if she were being drawn to Colorado by more than the strong engine of the train. Her heart was strangely pulled; there seemed to be almost a yearning. *Show me, Father. What would You have me to do?*

Sometime during the night, she awoke abruptly. Someone was having a whispered conversation outside her berth. She lay frozen, her heart pounding wildly.

"She doesn't know anything, I tell you!" She heard a man's loud whisper.

"Shut up! I'll take care of this," someone else growled softly. "It's not time yet! We need to wait and see if Oliver. . ."

The men's voices trailed off as they moved away. She blew out her breath, her body alternating cold and hot with fear. She could never forget that voice. What was he doing on this train? Was it possible that he had trailed her all the way from London, waiting for a chance to. . .to. . . She couldn't finish the thought. *Oh, God, please help me.*

The day dawned bright and clear, cheering Raine after her sleepless night. Looking around, she could hardly believe that the whispered conversation had really taken place. Was it all a bad dream? The ugly voice floated back to her. She shook her head. It wasn't a dream. *Maybe they weren't talking about me,* she tried to convince herself. She smiled wryly, knowing she was fooling herself if she believed that.

❧

She was unprepared for the feeling of homecoming that swept over her as she stepped off the platform in Colorado Springs. Drinking in the beauty of the land around her, her heart lifted in a song of praise. She had never seen country like this; it seemed that one could see for miles and miles in all directions—and there was not one cowboy or Indian in sight.

The snow-capped Rockies seemed to surround her, enfolding her in the wonder of their age-old beauty. Even the very air seemed to dance with life and expectancy, making her want to run and skip. Instead, she gathered her bags, letting the beauty and joy seep into her soul as she made her way down Pikes Peak Avenue. Waiting until the streetcar had gone past, she crossed the street to the telegraph office. Aunt Grace would never believe it, she thought with a smile. Colorado Springs was certainly no cow town.

She composed a short telegram, letting her aunt and uncle know she had arrived in one piece. The young clerk took the message, eyes widening slightly as he read her name. "If you're Raine Thomas, then I've got a telegram for you. Arrived yesterday."

She lifted her eyebrows in surprise, accepting the paper from the clerk.

RAINE STOP RECEIVED LETTER FROM BEN STOP
COPPER MINE INN STOP LOVE VIOLET

Her heart leapt. "Where is the Copper Mine Inn, please?"

The young man directed her to the inn, grinning and shaking her head as she tried to pay him. She hurried down the street in the direction he had pointed her, nearly running through the hotel's doors. In a breathless voice, she asked the clerk about Ben.

"Yes, Ma'am. Ben Thackeray had a room here. But I'm afraid he left yesterday."

"Left?" Had she missed him again?

"Yes'm. Don't know where he went. Sure left in a hurry."

Raine felt suddenly weary. "Do you have a room available?"

She made sure the door was locked securely before she lay across the hard bed. It felt good to be away from the constant rocking motion of the train. *Where has Ben gone,* she wondered, so discouraged that tears pooled in her eyes. She tried to think where he could have headed. Maybe he found Paul, and they both left for Boston.

She sat straight up at the thought, then slumped back down against the headboard. *Surely someone would have gotten the message to me if that had happened.* As it was, the telegram from Violet didn't say anything about him leaving. Raine's thoughts chased each other in circles until she finally fell asleep, the yearning to be held once again in Ben's arms was her last conscious thought.

She awoke feeling refreshed. Though her heart ached for Ben, she still felt a sense of anticipation as she prepared for the day. After all, she had come here to find her brother as well as Ben, so she might as well give it her best shot. Opening her Bible, her fingers turned directly to the often-read passage in Isaiah. Once again she gained strength as she read the promise God had given her in London. . . *I will bring the blind by a way that they have not known; I will lead them in paths that they knew not. . .* "Thank You for leading me thus far, Father," she prayed. "Please continue to guide me. . ."

She set out in determination. She sought out every place she could think of where someone might know her brother. After days of asking, she was almost ready to concede defeat. *God, I thought You led me here,* she cried one evening. Her feet were aching from so much walking, and the small amount of savings she had brought with her was dwindling along with her hope.

"Here I am in a strange town all by myself, without Ben—or Paul," she complained to the blank walls. "And with an evil man chasing me." True, she hadn't actually seen Red Hair since she escaped from him in London, but it had to have been him she heard that night on the train. She shuddered at the thoughts that were triggered in her mind just by recalling his voice. What were they talking about anyway? She was sure she had heard the name Oliver.

A new thought struck her. Could Paul still be living under an alias, even all this distance from Boston? Perhaps he was so afraid of being found, he wasn't using his own name at all. Maybe she had been going about this the wrong way.

She began making the rounds again the next day, this time describing Paul. Most people still shook their heads, but a few thought they might know someone who looked like the man she described. After a long discouraging day, she had met a rancher named Andrew, a shopkeeper named Bjorn, and two cowboys named Charlie, all of whom were very nice, but they weren't Paul.

Shoulders drooping, she let the tears fall freely. *I can't hear You anymore, Father. I thought I was trusting You, but I. . .* She was startled by a knock on the door. Hastily wiping away the tears, she opened the door.

The young clerk from the telegraph office shifted nervously from one foot to the other. "Ma'am? Sorry to bother you." He eyed her tear-streaked face. "I heard you was lookin' for your brother."

She nodded.

"Well, I might know somethin' about him."

Raine's heart leapt.

"I heard you explainin' what he looked like and, well, I think I've seen him before.

"You've seen Paul?" she whispered.

"I ain't for sure, ma'am. But I'm pretty good at noticin' things, and I noticed a man before that sounds like him."

"Why did you notice him? Is he a stranger?"

"Nah, he's not a stranger. He's a rancher that lives 'round here. I always notice him 'cause of that big ol' scar on his face."

Scar? Paul doesn't have a scar. . .or does he? Her mind flashed back to the first time she met Violet . . .*I was scared to death when I saw him come limping in, his head and face all covered in bandages. . .*Violet had said.

"Where did you say this man lives?" she asked cautiously.

"Don't know, ma'am. I jest know he lives south of here. Comes in for supplies now and then."

A rancher that lived to the south. Not a very big clue, but the best so far. "Thank you so much." She smiled at the young man. "I'll let you know if I find him."

The next morning found her driving southward. Setting her jaw, she stared out intently over the backs of her rented team. The man at the livery stable had objected when she asked to rent the team and wagon.

"I'll take my business elsewhere, then," she said stubbornly, turning to go. The man relented, eyeing her dubiously as she clambered up onto the seat. *I must look more confident than I feel,* she chuckled. In reality, she had only driven a team of horses once or twice in her life. But nothing was going to stop her from finding Paul after coming this far.

She stopped at the first ranch south of Colorado Springs, receiving a warm welcome, but no sign of Paul. The young ranch wife waved wistfully as Raine started down the road. She waved back, wishing she had time to stay and visit. It would be nice to have a friend here.

The drive to the next ranch was interminable. Surely she hadn't misunderstood the directions. She frowned. It was hot enough out here to be the fourth of July. September was never this hot in London, she thought as she felt the perspiration run down between her shoulder blades. Patting the moisture off her face as she finally neared the next ranch, she was startled to be greeted by shouting children, dogs yipping joyously at their heels. Why weren't these children in school?

She smiled at the children as she climbed down stiffly. Those wagon seats sure weren't made for comfort. "Is your mama home?" she asked.

"Yes'm." The oldest girl spoke up politely. "I'll go fetch her for ya."

The younger children grouped around Raine. In a flash, she was back at the Mission, surrounded by her children.

"Are you the teacher, Ma'am?" a small girl asked shyly.

"Naw, she's too pretty to be a teacher, Polly." The little girl's brother glared at her. "She's prob'ly a singer or somethin'."

Raine almost laughed out loud. "Well, I *am* a teacher, Polly," she said, smiling. "But I don't think I'm the one you're expecting." *That's why these children aren't in school at this time of year,* she thought, relieved. *They must be waiting for a new teacher.*

"Oh, yes, Ma'am. You are the one. Mama said. . ."

"What did Mama say?" A young woman with twinkling gray eyes and a pleasant face joined the small group.

"Mama! This is the teacher!"

"Oh?" The woman looked from her young daughter's animated face to Raine's bewildered expression. "Won't you come in for a cool drink, Miss. . .?"

"Thomas. Raine Thomas. Yes, I would like that." Raine found herself drawn to the young ranch family.

"I'm Emily Johnston." The woman introduced herself as she bustled around the kitchen, placing a plate of still-warm cookies on the table. "There. Help yourself." She sat down then, pushing her black hair back with a small hand. "Now, what was Polly jabbering about? She's my talker." She shook her head with a smile.

Raine responded immediately to Emily's warm smile. "I don't know, Emily. Your children greeted me when I pulled into the yard. Polly asked me if I was the teacher." She wrinkled her brow. "I *am* a teacher, but I'm not. . ."

Emily's eyes opened wide. "You really are a teacher?"

Raine nodded "Yes, but. . ."

"Do you love God?"

"Yes, but I. . ."

"Then you are the teacher."

"What?" Raine was shocked as Emily's eyes suddenly filled with tears.

"I've been praying and praying that God would send a teacher for my little ones. He must have sent you."

"But I'm not. . ."

"How did you know to come to our ranch?" Emily's eyes were sparkling with excitement now.

"Well, I. . ." Raine hated to disappoint the lovely woman in front of her, but. . . "Could you explain a little more of the situation to me?" she heard herself saying. What was she thinking? She couldn't just suddenly be "the teacher." What about Paul, not to mention Ben?

"Yes, yes of course. I was just so excited that you're finally here!" Emily smiled wistfully. "None of the children who live this far from town go to school, because there's not a school close enough for them to attend. We do our best with them at home, but I'm afraid it's not enough. We've all been praying that God would send a teacher to open a school close by, and here you are!"

What? Raine blinked. All this anticipation that she'd been feeling—could it be that God had a work for her to do in this beautiful country?

"I'll need to come back and talk to you about it some more, Emily," she found herself saying. "Could I come by next week?"

"Please do, Raine. I'll be waiting." Emily's face was as eager as little Polly's.

Raine waved as she turned to leave, the joy on the children's faces tugging at her heart. Shaken, she stopped the wagon as soon as she was out of sight of the Johnston ranch. A shiver of excitement quivered through her as the thought took hold. Could it be possible that God had brought her all the way to America to fulfill the call she knew He had placed on her life? She sat under the shade of a tree several minutes longer, considering the idea.

She had always sort of assumed that when she found Paul, they would both go back to England, and then. . .and then what? Paul and Christina would get married, and she would be alone. . .again. And what of Ben? Did he really love her? He had never mentioned marriage, though she had dreamed about the day she would become Mrs. Benjamin Luke Thackeray. But now. . .

Finally climbing back into the wagon, she realized that she had not even spoken with Emily about her real reason for coming to the ranch. Shrugging, she urged the horses on, making the rounds of a few more ranches before heading wearily back to town. If Paul was anywhere around here, she would find him. God would just have to take care of the rest.

By the time she pulled up in front of the livery stable, her backside ached so badly she wondered how she would walk the short distance back to the hotel. She handed the reins over to the stable hand, glaring at him as he flashed her a grin. She suppressed a groan as she crawled down from the wagon seat, silently thanking God the hotel wasn't too far.

The hot water soothed her aching muscles as she leaned back in the tub with a sigh. She hadn't found her brother, but maybe she had found something else. The small faces of Emily's children seemed to float in front of her eyes along with the steam. Her heart pulled her toward them, yet. . . *Paul! I have to find you. I can't just give up searching for you. Where are you?* Her heart was torn. *Lord Jesus, I feel Your presence, and I know You led me this far. But what do I do now?*

She crawled out of the tub and into bed, weary beyond belief. She felt like a dog chasing its own tail, her thoughts and prayers spinning in endless circles. Determined to continue the search for Paul, she tried pushing the faces of the children out of her mind. Finally falling into a fitful sleep, her dreams were filled with crying children, the faces of Emily's children mingling strangely with those of the children she had left behind at the Mission. She sat up in bed, suddenly wide awake, gripped with the conviction that God wanted her here in Colorado, teaching.

Dawn brightened the sky with changing hues of pink and yellow. Raine groaned and rolled over, putting the pillow over her head. She tried to tell herself that her experience in the night had been only a dream, but memories of other times that God had carefully led her flashed through her mind. She jumped up from the bed, nearly passing out from the sudden action.

She stomped over to the mirror and glared at her reflection, then she let her gaze roam to the large window. *It's not that I don't want to teach, but I thought You sent me here to find Paul, Father,* she argued weakly. Staring out the window several minutes longer, she received no more answer than the one she already knew in her heart.

Unable to deny it any longer, she blew out a long sigh. *I'll do it, Father,* she whispered.

❧

El Paso County, Colorado

Trixie snorted joyfully as she trotted through the gates of the Crooked P Ranch. "I agree with you wholeheartedly, Trix." Her weary rider patted her neck affectionately. "It's been a long trip home."

Tom slid stiffly from the saddle, turning Trixie's reins over to the waiting cowhand. "Thanks, Pete." He let his eyes rove over the familiar landscape as he trudged to the ranch house. "Looks the same to me," he muttered, disappointed. Somehow, he had expected something to be different when he arrived home.

What is it that I keep expecting to happen? Am I going

crazy? Pushing open the door with a sigh, the strange sense of urgency flooded over him again. Finally dropping to his knees, he cried out. "God, I can't stand it any longer. What would You have me to do?"

> ❧

A few days later, Tom sat nursing a cup of coffee at a back table in the Lantern Hotel, his thoughts a million miles away. He had gained a measure of peace since his prayer the night he returned from Santa Fe, but there was still something gnawing at him. *God, what do I need to do? I can't live with this feeling hanging over me constantly. . .*

"Heard 'bout the new schoolmarm since ya been back, Cox?"

The booming voice jolted Tom from his reverie. He raised his eyebrows questioningly over the rim of his mug.

"Purty little thing. Wants to start a school for the rancher's children." The man shook his head as he slid into the chair across from Tom. "Good idea, I reckon, but it sure seems a waste of a good woman, if ya know what I mean."

Tom smiled across at his friend. "Yeah, I know what ya mean, Jackson," he said, gently mocking the older man's western drawl. "Why don't you just get yourself a wife? Then you wouldn't have to worry yourself over every pretty new woman that comes to town."

"I'm tryin', I'm tryin'!" Jackson peered through his glasses at Tom. "Why don't you?" He asked pointedly.

Tom glanced away. "Been too busy," he muttered, even as a vision of beautiful blue eyes and golden curls grew in his mind. Pushing aside the painful memory, he stood. "Got to get back to work, Jackson. I've been gone too long."

Jackson nodded. "See ya, Cox. Watch out for that schoolmarm!"

Jackson's cackle followed Tom as he stepped out of the hotel door. Tom snorted. *Why would I be interested in a schoolmarm?* Striding into the general store, he picked up his supplies and headed back to the Crooked P, unaware of curious eyes watching his every move.

eleven

London, England

Ben tapped his foot impatiently, glancing at his watch. "I can't believe how long this is taking," he complained to himself.

Finally the door opened. "Mr. Rosen will see you now."

Ben sprang up in relief. Striding into the lawyer's office, he plunked the packet of papers down on the desk. "Here they are, Frank. What do I need to sign?"

The lawyer raised an eyebrow. "I still can't believe you're going through with this, Ben."

He shrugged. "I'm not going to change my mind, Frank. Just do what you need to do to make it legal."

Shaking his head, the young lawyer pulled out several forms. "You'll need to sign here. And here."

Ben sat back with a satisfied smile. Minutes later, he stood in front of the small house he had not seen in too many years. Tucking the papers into his breast pocket, he knocked firmly on the door.

"Hello, Father."

"Ben?" The older man threw the door open wide, his face lit with one of the only smiles Ben had ever seen there. He reached for his son eagerly as if to embrace him, then ended up patting him awkwardly on the shoulder. "Come in, come in!"

Ben stepped through the door. The house still smelled the same, a heavenly mixture of warm bread, freshly-washed clothes, and lavender sachets. Instantly he was ten years old again.

"Where's Mother?"

"I'll get her." His father started toward the kitchen, glancing back as if to make sure his son was still there. Ben took a deep breath, gathering his thoughts. Would she welcome him as his father had? He knew he must have hurt her by staying away so long. Perhaps she would refuse to see him.

He glanced up as she flew into the room. Her outstretched arms and radiant smile erased any doubts. Lifting her off her feet in an enormous hug, Ben felt tears spring into his eyes. "I've been wrong to stay away for so long," he began, looking from one parent to the other. "I've been bitter at you for the way I was raised." He sketched in the details of his life since they had parted ways, ending with a heartfelt plea. "Since I've accepted Christ as my Savior, I've realized that I need to ask your forgiveness for being angry and bitter against you. Will you forgive me?"

His father stared at him, tears flowing freely down his lined cheeks. "Ben—your mother and I are the ones who need to ask forgiveness. We have finally started to learn about the joy and peace that comes with a real relationship with Jesus Christ. Can you ever forgive us for leading you in the wrong way?"

☙

Ben pushed his plate away. "Mother, that was delicious. I can't eat another bite." His mother smiled, and Ben was struck once again by how much his parents had changed. He had accepted their offer for him to stay with them and had enjoyed the time immensely. But it was time to be heading back to where his heart told him he belonged.

"Father, Mother." They both looked up at his serious tone. "I have something to tell you. God has called me. . ." He described the yearning in his heart to serve as pastor to the hard-working ranchers near Colorado Springs. "Anyway, I sold my share of the shipping company." He paused, waiting for his words to sink in. "I want you to have half of the money."

☙

Ben had one more piece of business to take care of in London. When he accomplished his goal, the results were better than he had ever dared to hope. His heart was so light that he felt as though he could fly across the Atlantic. Now if only he could find Paul. . .

The next day found Ben on the deck of a ship, waving until his arm ached. The memory of his parents' faces as they stood arm in arm on the wharf was something he would treasure forever. There was a new sparkle in his mother's eye, and the look on his father's face could only be described as joyful.

What a blessing that they have truly come to know You, Father. Looking out across the calm waters of the Atlantic, his smile dissolved as he thought of a different time, a different ship. He remembered the way Raine's dusky green eyes had sparkled with laughter as they talked together on so many cool, moonlit evenings. He could almost feel her silky hair slipping through his fingers, the smell of her skin when he kissed her. . . *God, if there's any way, please give her back to me.*

Some days he could almost pretend that he had never given his heart away, but on days like this, the longing became unbearable. *I don't want to live my whole life without her, Lord Jesus. But I want to do Your will. If You mean for me to be alone, then I'm going to need Your strength. . .*

❧

"Raine's not here?" Ben stared at Raine's uncle John in consternation.

"I'm sorry, son. We tried to catch you before you left, but we were too late."

Ben shook his head in disbelief. "I must have just missed her. I can't believe she's been in Colorado all this time while I've been in London. If I'd come back to Boston before I left for England, at least I would have known. But I was in such a hurry to take care of my shipping business and have it done, that I left straight from New York. What a mess!"

"I have a feeling everything's going to work out just fine, Captain Ben. You do still love her, don't you?"

"More than I thought possible. And all this time I thought she had believed the worst about me." He grinned ruefully.

"Things sure can get twisted around, can't they?"

"That's for certain." John chuckled. "But I think things will untwist pretty quickly once you have that niece of mine in your arms again."

Ben felt the familiar longing press against his heart. "I hope so, John," he said softly. "I hope so."

☙

Raine sighed as she went to the door of her small hotel room. Would she ever have a moment of peace? Reluctantly pulling the door open a crack, she opened it wider when she recognized the young telegraph clerk. "Hello, Clay."

He was fairly vibrating with excitement. "I've seen him again, Miss Thomas! The man with the scar!"

Raine's heart leapt. "Where?"

"He was right here in town. I seen him eatin' at the Lantern Hotel. Then he went to the store, then left town." Clay hopped from foot to foot. "I heard another man call him 'Cox.'"

"Cox?" Raine wrinkled her brow. "But my brother's name is. . ." Her voice trailed off. *Of course. Grandfather's name was Oliver Cox.* "Thank you, Clay!" She smiled at him. "I think you've been a great help to me today."

Alone once again, Raine mulled over the new clue. If this man were Paul, how could she find out for sure? She grabbed her hat. She would just go and see for herself.

Her heart sank as the woman at the Lantern Hotel shook her head. "I remember seeing a man that sounds like the one you're after, but I surely don't know his name." The motherly woman looked at Raine kindly. "Are you in trouble, child?"

"Trouble?" Raine shook her head. Suddenly, the color flooded to her cheeks as she realized what the woman meant. "Oh no, Ma'am." She hastened to clear herself. "I'm looking for my brother."

Covering her flaming cheeks with her hands, Raine missed the look of compassion in the woman's eyes. "Well, the best of luck to you, child."

Raine turned to go. Almost to the door, she looked up just

in time to avoid crashing into an enormous man. "I beg your pardon," she murmured, her eyes glued to the man's chest in embarrassment.

"Not at all, not at all, little lady," he boomed. "You're the new schoolmarm, aren't you?"

She jerked her gaze back up to the man's twinkling eyes. "Yes, I am. But how—?"

The man laughed. "Aw, I make it my business to know just about everything going on in this town. In fact, I couldn't help but hearing part of your conversation with Nancy here." He gestured to the woman Raine had just spoken to. "I reckon I could tell you a bit about the man you're looking for."

Raine stared at him. "You know Paul?" She whispered.

"I don't know about any Paul, but I do know the man you described to Nancy. Name's Tom Cox. Owns a ranch south of here. Why is it you're looking for Tom?"

He certainly isn't shy, she thought, amused. "Actually, I'm not certain that it's Tom I want to see, Mr. . .?"

"Jackson. Just Jackson, no Mister. Why are you asking for Tom if you don't know if you want to see him?"

She sighed. "It's a long story, Mr.—Jackson."

Jackson took the hint and stopped probing. "Well, it was mighty fine to meet you. I've got to get going now, myself."

Raine put out a small hand. "Thank you for telling me about Tom," she said sincerely.

Jackson shook her hand until she was sure it would fall off. "Most welcome, ma'am. Most welcome."

Back in her room, Raine stood staring out her window, deep in thought. The growing twilight mimicked her thoughts—fuzzily outlined ideas, barely discernable theories swathed in shadows. *Tom Cox, Cox, Cox.* She had been unable to think of little else, the man's name beating a rhythm in her brain.

She lay down with a sigh, images of a dark-haired man with a scar merging with loving thoughts of a tall, golden-haired man. Restless, she tossed back and forth. "Ben, please come to me," she mumbled as her dreams became more real. "I need you. No one will believe me that Paul Thomas is my brother

. . .Paul Thomas has a scar. . .Tom Cox, Paul T. . ."

She woke with a start, her dream still vivid in her mind. She knew suddenly without a doubt that Tom was short for Thomas and since Cox was their grandfather's name; it had to be Paul. She hugged the pillow to her chest, too excited to go back to sleep. *Surely I can find his ranch now that I know his name,* she reasoned. *Maybe Jackson will help me in the morning. Maybe he even knows where the ranch is.* She made joyful plans, whiling away the long hours of the night. The only pain left to mar her joy was Ben's absence.

❧

"Well, I reckon I could spare some time to drive a pretty woman out to the Crooked P Ranch." Jackson was delighted with Raine's request. "And even if that ol' Tom Cox isn't your brother, I reckon he wouldn't complain any about having the new schoolmarm pay him a visit."

Raine smiled in embarrassment. Jackson was a nice enough man, but he was so—big. Everything about him was big, from his boots to his voice.

"I'm ready to go now, if you are," she said politely.

"Well, just climb right up here into the wagon seat then, little lady. We'll be out to the Crooked P before you know it." He clucked to the horses, waving his hat proudly at every man on the street. "They just wish they were so lucky to have the schoolmarm ride with one of them," he boomed to Raine.

Raine doubted that it really mattered to anyone who Jackson was driving around in his wagon. Nevertheless, she ducked her head slightly, cringing under the curious stares of everyone they passed. Soon they were out of town, and she let out a relieved sigh. "How far is it to Paul's—I mean Tom's ranch?"

"Little ways yet," was Jackson's cheerful reply. "Aren't those mountains about the prettiest sight you ever laid eyes on?"

Raine had to agree that the beauty of this country was breathtaking. At the moment, though, all her thoughts were focused on what awaited her at the Crooked P Ranch. Could it really be possible, after all these years? She could hardly imagine being in her brother's strong arms once again, seeing his precious face. . .and just wait until she wrote and told Papa! What a wonderful. . .

". . .and that over there is one of those pesky little prairie dogs." Raine's thoughts were jerked back to the present as Jackson waved a hand in her direction. "They dig those little burrows, then the horses step in them and break their leg. Yep, those prairie dogs sure are a nuisance. Kinda cute little critters, though."

Raine looked around. Sure enough, there were little mounds of dirt dotting the prairie as far as the eye could see. Anxious prairie dogs stood up on tiny hind legs, prepared to dive for safety at the slightest hint of danger.

Jackson glanced at her. "You must be pretty excited to see Tom again," he said, his voice as near to quiet as he could manage.

Raine nodded, scanning the prairie as if she would see Paul suddenly materialize before her. "Yes, it's been a long time, Jackson." Her voice quivered as a sudden thought assailed her. "I just hope he wants to see me."

Jackson's voice dropped even lower. "Aw, Miss Thomas. Don't you worry. That old rascal has been pining away about something ever since I knew him. Never would tell me about it. I bet he's just dying to see you."

"I hope so," Raine said quietly.

ъ

Tom squinted at the small cloud of dust in the distance. *Must be Jess coming over to drive those stray calves of his home,* he decided. Swinging up on Trixie's broad back, Tom rode out to meet his neighbor. Drawing closer to the dusty cloud, he realized that it wasn't a lone rider as he had expected, but a wagon. He squinted at it, frowning as he recognized the driver. *Jackson! Why in the world is he coming out here in the middle of the day?* Usually only bad news could tear a rancher away from a hard day's work; visiting was reserved for evenings when the work was done.

Tom nudged Trixie into a gallop, his heart beating faster in spite of himself. Maybe someone had finally fallen into that dry well near the Baxter's. He knew it was going to happen one of these days. Or maybe it was Grandma Lydia. The dear old saint had been barely clinging to life for days now. . .

"I brought the schoolmarm out to meet ya, Tom!"

Tom barely heard Jackson's shout over the pounding of Trixie's hooves, but his heart slowed its frantic pace as he noticed Jackson's smile. Yanking Trixie to a halt, Tom stared at the woman sitting next to Jackson. Her face swam before his eyes as a loud rushing filled his ears. He shook his head in disbelief, then raised his eyes slowly to meet hers.

"Raine?"

She was out of the wagon almost before he could dismount. Throwing her arms around his neck, she wept until there were no more tears. "Oh Paul! It's really you! Thank God I finally found you!"

Paul let his sister cry, his own tears falling thick and fast onto her hair. Holding her tightly, he felt the last of the restlessness in his soul all but vanish. All the waiting, the longing; this was what his heart had needed. Pushing her away gently, he gazed lovingly at her face. She had grown into a beautiful woman since he had last seen her. He took in the short hair, the beautiful eyes filled with joy and yet somehow marked with sadness. "It's time for us to talk, little sister," he said huskily.

Raine nodded, too full of emotion to speak. Suddenly remembering Jackson, she turned to find that he had tactfully slipped away.

Paul helped Raine mount Trixie. Swinging up on the patient horse, Paul turned her toward the house. "Home, girl," he murmured.

Raine clasped her brother's waist tightly as they rode, laying her head on his strong back. *Thank You, Father.*

&

"So—start at the beginning, Ray." Raine was ensconced in the only comfortable chair Paul owned. He sat on a stool at her feet, his face eager.

"Well, first of all, you have to understand that I didn't

receive any of your letters, except one. That's partly why it took me so long to find you."

"What?" Paul jumped to his feet. "I must have written you a hundred letters since I first left home. I finally gave up writing about the time I came out here. I didn't dare. But how could you not. . ." His voice trailed off as understanding dawned. "It was Papa, wasn't it?" he asked flatly.

"I'm afraid so, Paul. All that time I couldn't understand why you didn't write me any letters, and Papa was destroying them all before I could see them." Raine's smile was sad. "But he is sorry, Paul. He begged me to forgive him."

Paul shook his head. "I thought that he had poisoned you against me, and that's why you never answered any of my letters." He turned his head so that Raine could not see the tears shimmering in his eyes. "Back in Boston—and even here in Colorado—I checked my mail box every week, hoping somehow that you still loved me and cared about me."

Raine slipped from her chair, gathering her brother into her arms like a small child. "I never stopped loving you, Paul. I thought I would die of loneliness when you left."

"Me too," he whispered.

She wiped the tears from her face. "I'm never going to get through the whole story if we don't stop crying!" She laughed shakily.

Many minutes and many tears later, Paul sat looking at his sister in amazement. "You've grown into a strong woman, Raine Thomas," he said quietly. He frowned. "Tell me again about the man who abducted you."

Raine described the man once again, watching as her brother's face paled. "I can't believe he would go that far." Paul gritted his teeth. "I'm sure he's the same man who has been after me, Raine. His name is Dag."

"You know who he is?"

Paul nodded grimly. "I know all too well. He tried to kill me." Determined not to dwell on the subject, he made an effort to smile at Raine. "We can talk about that later. I know you have a few questions of your own that I need to answer."

She sensed his need to change the topic of conversation. "Yes, I have quite a few questions that need answering, as a matter of fact," she replied with mock sternness.

He flashed her a boyish grin. "It's not that bad is it?"

"You didn't make it very easy on me, big brother. What was the idea of telling everyone we were married?"

Paul smiled at the look of reproach on her face. "Seriously, I never dreamed it would make trouble for you. I didn't do it purposely at first." He shook his head, remembering.

Ben took a long look at the photograph. "So this is your girl," he said slowly. "She's beautiful."

Paul opened his mouth to correct Ben, then snapped it shut. For some reason, it didn't seem like a bad idea to let Ben assume that Raine was his fiancée. He didn't know Ben well then, and he wasn't sure he liked the look on Ben's face as he gazed at the photograph of Raine. Then somehow, the lie had mushroomed.

"I didn't always do the right thing at that point in my life, Raine." Paul hung his head. "After I let Ben believe that you and I were engaged, it got easier to lie about it. I didn't intend for it to turn into such a big thing, but I guess I'm a coward."

Raine stared at her brother in confusion. "But why?"

"I figured that if I let it slip to the other crew members that I was married, maybe they wouldn't be so rough on me." He looked at Raine pleadingly. "I didn't mean to cause you trouble. It's just that it was hard enough to stay away from the tavern, and when my fellow sailors thought I was married, they didn't pressure me so much about, well, the girls." Paul ended his sentence in embarrassment.

Raine's eyes softened. "I can understand that, Paul. But Violet. . ."

"That was another matter altogether," he admitted. "She just assumed. . .and I never bothered to correct her. I guess after what I'd been through, it just seemed like a nice change, me a respectable married man instead of. . ." He flushed.

"But you did know that Lucinda revealed the father's true identity after the child was born? Surely you heard. . ."

The look of relief on her brother's face was so profound, Raine knew he hadn't known until that moment.

"Oh, Paul. All this time. . ."

"But Papa. . .?"

"He was too guilty himself to be able to reconcile with you. I know that now. At the time, I thought you would come back as soon as you found out that you were absolved. I guess it just made it all the harder when I didn't hear from you. Oh Paul, I thought you were dead!" She finished with a sob, recalling those dark days. "Thank God He kept His hand on you all these years."

Paul nodded soberly. "I'll say amen to that." Then he paused. "Is that why you thought I stayed away? Because of Lucinda and the baby?"

She nodded. "Of course. Then when I found out your true identity, I assumed you were angry with Papa for hiding it from you. I didn't know anything about the espionage until Geoff told me."

"You know?" Paul stared at her. "Geoff—?"

Raine explained about her meeting with Geoff.

"So that's what happened." Paul shook his head. "I can't believe he's alive! Of course I forgive him—I know he had no idea what he was getting me into. I just wish the whole mess would end now."

"We've found each other. That's what counts. I promised Papa I'd bring you home to him."

Paul shook his head. "I can't. I can't go back to England. Why do you think I talk like an American now?"

It was true; she had noticed that he had wiped away all traces of a British accent. She shook her head.

"I'm not a free man, Raine." He set his jaw. "I won't be free until my name is cleared. I ran away to escape being hung along with those other fellows. That's why I never told anyone when I left for Colorado. Dag had found me in Boston, and I knew I had to get away. I even had all my mail sent to Denver, just in case he is still hunting me. It's a bit far to go to the post office, but I didn't want to lead anyone straight to my door."

She wanted to weep, but she pulled herself together.

"I hated to sneak away from Boston like that," Paul continued, "but I had to. That big galoot of a sailor was after me again, and I had to. . ."

Raine interrupted, "Is that who you meant when you said you were being pursued?"

"Yes. I'm so sorry you had to go through what you did. I never dreamed he would involve you too."

"But what was he talking about, Paul? Why did he want those papers that you had put in the safe deposit box?"

"Because they proved his guilt and my innocence." Paul stared out the window. When he turned back to Raine, she was shocked at the pain revealed in his eyes. "It's another long story, Raine. The gist of it is that I made a mess of things once again. And Christina. . ."

He fell silent.

"What happened, Paul?" Raine prompted gently.

He stood up, pacing in agitation. "One of the chaps that was accused of smuggling had gotten off from lack of evidence. He showed up on Ben's ship, as a crew member. I suspected that he was still up to no good—and he thought it was a big joke that I was still wanted for the crime for which he had escaped conviction. He kept threatening to notify the authorities in England, turn me in. But then I began to suspect that he was still up to his old tricks. While we were in port at Boston, I searched his cabin and I found papers hidden beneath his mattress. The papers were in code, but they were easy enough for me to decipher. They proved that I had never been involved in the espionage ring back in England—and they also proved Dag's guilt. I should have gone straight to Ben with the information, but I didn't. I wanted to be a hero. And then it was too late."

He sighed and fell silent for a moment before he continued. "I had spoken to an agent in New York. He promised me that if what I said was true, there would be hefty reward for my part in Dag's capture. I already had enough evidence to convict him of his part in the spy ring back in England, but I wanted proof that he was still up to his sneaky tricks. Anyway, I was going to go on one more voyage and see what I could catch him at, then be done with it. I would collect the reward, pay off Christina's agreement with her employer, and we'd head west together."

Raine nodded, totally absorbed as the pieces of the puzzle finally fell into place.

"I was going to whisk Christina away from that miserable hole she has to work in, and the two of us would start a new life together."

"But?"

"But it didn't work out that way. I was getting pretty cocky, and I think Dag started to become suspicious of me. Anyway, someone told Ben that I was involved in something underhanded. At the same time, Dag threatened to turn me into the English authorities, and I countered by telling him that I had information that proved my innocence and his guilt. That was my biggest mistake. I should have gone to Ben instead."

"Oh, Paul."

"I could tell Ben wondered whether to trust me, but he didn't say anything, and I thought I would wait 'til the thing was over and done with and then I'd tell him."

So that's why Ben had seemed ambivalent toward Paul sometimes. "So Ben suspected the worst."

He shrugged. "I suppose so. After the *Aramathea* sank, I determined that no matter what, I would not be blamed for something I didn't do. I decided rather than risk going through what I had gone through before, I would just run away. Like I said, I'd been planning to go out west anyway, and I figured Ben would get the locket to you, so you'd know where I was. I hoped Ben would be able to clear my name for me, and then get word to me when it was safe to come back east. And I hoped you'd find me. . .maybe follow me."

Raine's heart felt as though it would break when she thought of Paul's loneliness and pain all these years, but she forced herself to say cheerfully, "Well, I did. It just took me a little longer than you'd thought, thanks to the sea water that destroyed most of your message in the locket."

Paul shook his head ruefully. "I thought I was being so clever. I knew I'd lost Christy. . .but I'd always hoped I hadn't lost you too. I made plans to head west as soon as I returned."

"But where does Christina fit in?"

Paul's eyes took on a soft light. "Ah, Christina. We were so happy. We had big plans to come out west and live happily ever after on a huge ranch."

"What happened, Paul?" Raine felt her brother's pain as if it were her own. He closed his eyes. "She was so beautiful. I can still see her standing there waving to me as we left the harbor."

Paul turned wistfully from the railing, only to meet the blazing eyes of Dag.

"You're right about this being your last voyage, Oliver," Dag had whispered ominously. "I'll see to that."

Paul felt a quick chill of fear flutter through him, quickly replaced by anger. "Don't threaten me, Dag. Go do your job." Paul's voice was cool, but the look in the other sailor's eyes sent fear racing through him.

He watched Dag closely throughout the voyage, finding himself relaxing as each uneventful day slipped by. Then, waking to the shrill sound of the warning alarms and the frantic cries of passengers that fateful night, all thoughts of Dag disappeared.

He shook his head. "It all happened so fast, Ray. I gave the locket to Ben, with the message inside that would tell you go see Violet and then look for me in Colorado, and then we began doing what we could to make sure everyone got into a lifeboat safely. I was helping a young woman with a baby into the lifeboat, when I felt a horrible sensation crawl up my spine. I whirled around, but it was too late."

Raine was stunned. "He pushed you off the ship?"

Paul nodded, his face haggard. "After he slashed my face with his dagger. I think he was aiming for my heart, but I ducked. . .anyway, while I was still reeling from the blow, he gave me a shove over the railing. I clung to him, tried to tell him it wouldn't do any good, since the papers that proved his guilt were safe in a bank, but it was useless of course. I felt myself drop, and the floats in my life preserver caught me under the chin when I hit the water. I was lucky not to have broken my neck. When I came to, I was too far away to get aboard any of the lifeboats." He brushed at the moisture forming in his eyes. "That was the first time I had called out to God in a long, long time."

Raine felt tears prick her own eyes. "How did you make it back to Boston?"

He smiled sadly. "I guess God didn't think it was my time to go yet. Another ship picked me up at dawn. I had pretty much decided I was going to die out there, but here I am."

"I can't believe all of this, Paul." Raine shook her head in amazement. "So then you went back to Violet's, and she nursed you back to health. Then what? Why didn't you let Ben know you had survived? And what about Christina? Why did you leave her?"

Paul shrugged. "I don't know. I was kind of confused, maybe from the blow I took on my head." He stared out the window again. "I was feeling some better and decided to go see Christina. She stared at me like I was a ghost when I hobbled in."

Paul smiled as he remembered the look on her face. "She had heard about the ship and assumed I was dead when I was not brought back in with the other crew members. We decided to get married as soon as I was well.

"And, I was taking a walk a day or two later. Violet always got after me to get some fresh air."

Raine smiled, picturing the kindly old lady ordering her brother around.

"Anyway, I saw him, Raine."

"Who, Dag?"

"Yes. Maybe it was an accident that I ran into him, maybe he was checking to make sure I was really dead. Anyway, I knew he now knew that I had survived, and he was after me. I was sure that sooner or later he would try to kill me again.

I was afraid he would even hurt Christina." His forehead wrinkled. "Actually, there were two men following me. I have no idea who the second man was, and I never saw him at the same time I saw Dag."

"He wasn't out to harm you, Paul." Raine smiled at his startled look. "Papa had a man trailing you."

Paul stared at his sister incredulously. "Why?"

"He still loves you, Paul. He is longing for your forgiveness."

Paul opened his mouth to speak, then snapped it shut, shaking his head in disbelief.

"Anyway, so you left Boston in the middle of the night to escape from Dag. Why didn't you take Christina with you?" Raine changed the subject tactfully, sensing that Paul was not yet ready to talk about their father.

"I panicked, Ray. I knew by then that Dag was serious about killing me, since he had already tried once. I left that night, intending to either sneak back to get Christina in a few days or send for her to come to me."

Raine winced at the pain written across her brother's face.

"By the time I arrived in Colorado, I had myself convinced that I was worthless. My name was muddied, my father accused me of something that he was guilty of, my sister hated me, and a man was trying to kill me. On top of all that, I was a liar and a drunk who had turned his back on God. I couldn't ask someone like Christina to share life with me."

Paul stared at his sister wistfully. "All these years, I've been hating myself for leaving her, hating myself for making such a mess of my life, trying to get up enough courage to contact her again and see if she still loves me. Finally, I decided that by now she has found someone else."

Raine dropped her gaze, feeling like an intruder as she witnessed the raw agony in her brother's eyes. "Do you remember the time I told you that Christina would wait for you until the end of the world?"

He raised his head to stare at his sister.

She smiled. "She's still waiting, Paul."

twelve

Raine lay awake for hours, reliving the reunion with Paul. She had to smile as she recalled the look on his face when she had handed him the small package from Christina. He had not opened it, but held it in his hands lovingly. She guessed he would open it in private, and she didn't begrudge him that at all.

She sighed. There were still so many unanswered questions. Was Dag still tracking Paul? She was loathe to mention her suspicions to her brother, but she could not forget the whispered conversation she had heard on the train, nor the chill of fear it still sent down her spine whenever she thought of it. True, she had seen no sign of the red-haired sailor in the weeks she had been in Colorado, but. . .

Father, thank You for finally leading me to Paul! You are so good to me. Please show me how to minister to him, Lord. His soul is still so wounded. Give me wisdom, Father, and protect us from this evil man Dag. And Father, please bring Ben back to me!

Despite her joy of finding Paul, lonely tears escaped down Raine's cheeks as she ached for Ben's strong arms around her. *Please come back to me, my love. . .*

❧

"Crooked P Ranch sure is a busy place these days, I'll say." Jackson said when Ben asked him to drive him out to the ranch.

"Why do you say that, Jackson?" Ben asked absently, his mind on other matters.

"Well, first I took that pretty little schoolmarm out there a couple of days ago. Then just this morning I took a big ol' feller out there. Said he was an old friend of Tom's. Didn't look very friendly to me, but I reckon that's none of my business."

Ben glanced at Jackson. Something made him ask, "What did the man look like?"

"Big ol' feller, like I said. Hair as orange as carrots and a big tattoo on his hand."

Dag again. Ben found it hard to believe that the man would trail Raine all the way from London, but it had to be him. He blew out his breath.

"Jackson, I think we're going to run into some trouble at the Crooked P. Are you still game to drive me out there?"

The old rancher's eyes sparkled. He patted his hip. "Got my trusty pistol right here, Mr. Ben. Let's go."

Ben perched tensely on the edge of the wagon seat, thinking back over the past few weeks. Raine's aunt and uncle had received a letter from Raine the same day Violet had received one from Paul. Violet had smiled through her tears. "He finally wrote! Paul is alive!"

Ben had read Paul's and Raine's letters, filled with joy, wishing only that there had been a letter for him. . . A jolt of the wagon brought Ben back to the present.

"Just one of them prairie dog holes," Jackson mumbled.

Ben stared at the rolling plains, praying for wisdom. "All right, this is our plan, Jackson. When we get about a mile away from the ranch house, we're going to have to abandon the wagon and go the rest of the way on foot."

Ben related the rest of the plan, fear threatening to cloud his good sense as he realized what they might be stepping into. He took a deep breath. "If you're a praying man, now's the time to pray, Jackson," he said grimly.

Grasping his pistol tightly, Ben closed his eyes for a moment, taking deep breaths. Abruptly, his eyes flew open. *I will never leave you, nor forsake you.* The words of Scripture came from nowhere, flooding through him like great calming waves. "Thank You, God," he whispered.

Jackson jerked the wagon to a halt behind a small rise. "Ranch house is just over that hill," he whispered. "Are you ready?"

Ben nodded. "This is it." The two men swung silently to the

ground. Ben helped the older man tether the team, praying that the horses wouldn't whinny and give away their presence. The men parted ways with a grim handshake. "Remember, if we can just make it inside the house, we'll be able to pull this off. God go with you, Jackson."

Crawling quietly through the tall prairie grass, Ben's heart was pounding crazily. He and Jackson had decided to take separate routes to the ranch house in hopes that if one was seen, the other would still have a chance. *Please, Father, don't let us be too late.* He shook his head, refusing to imagine what was happening behind the closed door of the ranch house.

⁂

Raine sat motionless, tears flowing steadily down her cheeks and soaking into the rag that was gagging her. She longed to cover her ears, but could not get her hands loose from the tightly-tied knots. She winced as another cry sounded from the bedroom. *Father, please don't let him kill Paul! Please deliver us somehow!*

It had all happened in a flash. Raine awoke to Dag standing over her, a knife at her throat. He had forced her into the kitchen where Paul already sat, ashen-faced. Dag bound Raine to a chair, then gleefully waved the dog-eared photo of Raine in front of his captives. "I always knew this would lead me to you, Oliver. You thought everything was lost in the shipwreck, didn't you?"

Paul blanched.

"Well, it just so happens that your precious captain left this behind in his hurry to do his duty. All I had to do was wait until he led me to the beautiful lady in this photograph." Dag sneered at Raine. "And sure enough, she led me straight to you. It took awhile, but that doesn't really matter much anymore, does it?"

Raine stared at the man's twisted face. His eyes blazed, and she realized then that it was madness she saw gleaming in his eyes. He had yielded so long to his obsession of hatred and revenge that he had become insane. Why else would he have pursued her and Paul so long and so far?

Whirling suddenly, Dag untied Paul without another word and led him into the bedroom. For twenty minutes now there had been curses and blows intermingled with unspeakable cries as Dag struck Paul repeatedly. She stared out the window helplessly, not even knowing how to pray. Surely God wouldn't let them die at the hands of this man, after bringing them this far.

She watched the midmorning sun shimmering on the plains. Watched as the ranch hands poured out of the bunkhouse and headed in the direction of the corrals, too far away to hear the commotion going on in the ranch house. How odd that everything seemed to be going on as normal, except inside this house. Her thoughts drifted as she tried not to think of what might happen next.

What was that? Raine's eye had caught a flash of movement just above the window sill. She watched the spot intently, finally rewarded as she saw another swift flutter of . . .what was it? Cautiously thumping her feet once on the floor, she kept her eyes glued on the window.

ะ

Ben knelt beneath the window, his blood pounding in his temples. Taking a deep breath, he started to rise when he heard a small thump.

Just do it, Thackeray, he commanded himself. Springing up, he started as he met Raine's frightened gaze. He collapsed under the window. *She's still alive! Thank You, God!* Even in his quick glance into the room, he knew that she was alone, at least for the moment. Standing up cautiously, he mouthed the words. "Where is he?"

Raine jerked her head toward the bedroom, her eyes now aglow with hope.

"I love you." Ben mouthed, rewarded as he saw her eyes soften in answer. Ducking back down, he flattened himself against the wall, inching his way around to the other side of the house. His heart leapt as he saw Jackson already there, listening intently with his head pressed against the wall.

"God is truly with us, Jackson," Ben said softly. He told him of finding Raine alone in the kitchen. "I think we can make it into the house through that door." He nodded toward the kitchen door. "Ol' Dag is swearing so loudly he won't hear us anyway." As if on cue, the big sailor let loose a stream of foul language, followed by several loud crashes.

Ben grimaced. "We'd better hurry!"

He peered cautiously through the kitchen window, relieved that Raine was still alone. Stealthily, the men slid through the door. Ben hurriedly cut the ropes that bound Raine. Jerking the filthy rag out of her mouth, he couldn't help himself and brushed a tender kiss across her swollen lips.

Taking a swift inventory of the minuscule kitchen, he pushed her toward the pantry. "Get in there and don't come out until I tell you it's safe," he whispered, giving her a longing glance.

❧

Raine sat silently amid the jars, cans, and bottles, praying as never before. *God, protect Ben and Jackson. Show them what to do. Protect Paul, please Father. Deliver us from this horrible man. . .Jesus, help us!* She covered her head involuntarily as a shot rang out. Hearing nothing more, she stood up carefully, but her still numb legs betrayed her. Her knees buckled, and she sent a shower of jars to the floor as she tried to keep from falling. She stood clinging to the shelf, her heart in her mouth as she heard heavy footsteps approaching. She stifled a scream as the door jerked open, then suddenly she was in Ben's arms. Weak with relief, she clung to him tightly.

"Shh, it's all over now, kitten. You're safe," he murmured comfortingly.

"Don't ever leave me again, Ben," she sobbed, the emotions of the lonely weeks and months pouring out uncontrollably.

"I'm right here, honey." Ben smoothed her hair back tenderly. "I love you, Raine," he whispered.

Raine nodded her head against his chest, relishing the feeling of safety that came from being in his arms at last.

"Hey, little sister. Don't I get a hug too?" Raine jerked away from Ben at the sound of Paul's weak voice.

"Oh, Paul!" The tears flowed anew at the sight of her brother's battered face. "What did he do to you?"

"I've had worse." Paul tried to smile. "I just don't have Violet to cluck over me this time."

"Well, you have me," Raine said firmly. "If you think Violet was tough, you haven't seen anything yet."

"Yes, Ma'am." Paul rolled his eyes. "I assume you know what you're getting yourself in for, Ben?"

"What?" Raine felt the blood rise to her cheeks. "What do you mean by that?"

Paul smiled. "I've got eyes in my head, Ray, even if they are a little swollen at the moment. When are you two going to tie the knot?"

Raine's cheeks grew even rosier. She glanced at Ben. "Well, I. . ." She jumped as someone behind her cleared his throat loudly.

"Guess I'll be getting back to town, now." Jackson grinned. "Looks like ya'll don't need me any more."

Ben smiled as he watched Jackson saunter away. "That man was sent by God for us today," he said seriously. "I wouldn't be surprised if He's got some big plans for him."

"Well, I know someone who has some big plans for you, Captain." Paul grinned at his sister. "Just get me a cold rag for my poor face, then go take care of Ben, Ray."

Raine obeyed her brother with a sparkle in her eye. After seeing him tucked in bed to her satisfaction, she turned to Ben shyly. Ben smiled down at her, then turned to Paul.

"I almost forgot! A lovely young lady in Boston asked me to deliver this to you." He flipped a letter onto Paul's bed, smiling at the eagerness on Paul's face. "And by the way— you're a free man now. The authorities took the information in those papers you left me and put it together with clues they'd received from other sources. They reached the conclusion that you were innocent of espionage." He grinned at the dazed look on Paul's face. "I said I'd pass this along to you."

Paul took the official-looking paper and nodded absently, but he was already opening the letter from Christina.

Ben smiled at Raine, offering her his arm. "Shall we leave him alone now?"

She returned his smile and nodded.

Once outside the kitchen door, Ben couldn't stand it any longer. Drawing Raine eagerly into his arms, he kissed her deeply.

She clung to him, heady with joy. "This is where I belong," she murmured, snuggling deeper into his arms.

Ben held her tenderly, his heart overflowing. "I love you, Raine Thomas."

"And I love you." She looked up at him, her eyes sparkling with joy. "I missed you so much, Ben. I prayed and prayed that God would bring you back to me."

Ben nodded. "I prayed the same thing. I was so hurt when I thought you didn't trust me. I came out here to find Paul, but instead, God found me."

Raine stared at his joyful face. "What do you mean, Ben? I thought you had already given your life to Christ in Boston."

"I did, Raine," he assured her. "It's just that I didn't know what God wanted me to do with the rest of my life." He hesitated. "I would love to ask you to be my wife, Raine, but I have to be honest with you. God has called me to stay here in Colorado and start a church for the ranchers."

Raine could only smile at him.

"Could you live here the rest of your life, Raine?" His voice was low.

Raine finally found her voice. "Ben," she whispered, "God has called me to stay here, too. I'm going to teach at the school for the rancher's children!"

Ben looked at her wonderingly. He took her face into his hands, staring tenderly into her beautiful eyes. "Then, will you spend the rest of your life with me, Raine, and be my wife?"

Raine's yes was joyful and full of promise, for she knew that God would continue to lead her along unfamiliar paths, making the crooked ways straight.

A Letter To Our Readers

Dear Reader:

In order that we might better contribute to your reading enjoyment, we would appreciate your taking a few minutes to respond to the following questions. When completed, please return to the following:

Rebecca Germany, Managing Editor
Heartsong Presents
PO Box 719
Uhrichsville, Ohio 44683

1. Did you enjoy reading *Along Unfamiliar Paths*?
   ❑ Very much. I would like to see more books
      by this author!
   ❑ Moderately
      I would have enjoyed it more if _____

   _____

2. Are you a member of **Heartsong Presents**? ❑Yes ❑No
   If no, where did you purchase this book? _____

   _____

3. What influenced your decision to purchase this
   book? (Check those that apply.)

   ❑ Cover   ❑ Back cover copy

   ❑ Title   ❑ Friends

   ❑ Publicity   ❑ Other_____

4. How would you rate, on a scale from 1 (poor) to 5
   (superior), the cover design? _____

5. On a scale from 1 (poor) to 10 (superior), please rate the following elements.

    ___Heroine   ___Plot

    ___Hero   ___Inspirational theme

    ___Setting   ___Secondary characters

6. What settings would you like to see covered in **Heartsong Presents** books?_____

_____

_____

7. What are some inspirational themes you would like to see treated in future books?_____

_____

_____

8. Would you be interested in reading other **Heartsong Presents** titles?   ❑ Yes   ❑ No

9. Please check your age range:
   ❑ Under 18   ❑ 18-24   ❑ 25-34
   ❑ 35-45   ❑ 46-55   ❑ Over 55

10. How many hours per week do you read? _____

Name _____

Occupation_____

Address_____

City_____ State_____ Zip _____

A Romantic Collection
of Inspirational Novellas

Discover how two words, so softly spoken, create one glorious life with love's bonds unbroken. *I Do,* a collection of four all-new contemporary novellas from **Heartsong Presents** authors, will be available in May 1998. What better way to love than with this collection written especially for those who adore weddings. The book includes *Speak Now or Forever Hold Your Peace* by Veda Boyd Jones, *Once Upon a Dream* by Sally Laity, *Something Old, Something New* by Yvonne Lehman, and *Wrong Church, Wrong Wedding* by Loree Lough. These authors have practically become household names to romance readers, and this collection includes their photos and biographies.   (352 pages, Paperbound, 5" x 8")

·········· Presents ··········

Great Inspirational Romance at a Great Price!

Heartsong Presents books are inspirational romances in contemporary and historical settings, designed to give you an enjoyable, spirit-lifting reading experience. You can choose wonderfully written titles from some of today's best authors like Peggy Darty, Sally Laity, Tracie Peterson, Colleen L. Reece, Lauraine Snelling, and many others.

When ordering quantities less than twelve, above titles are $2.95 each.
Not all titles may be available at time of order.

Heartsong Presents
Love Stories Are Rated G!

That's for godly, gratifying, and of course, great! If you lo[ve] a thrilling love story, but don't appreciate the sordidness of son[e] popular paperback romances, **Heartsong Presents** is for you. [In] fact, **Heartsong Presents** is the *only inspirational romance bo[ok] club*, the only one featuring love stories where Christian faith [is] the primary ingredient in a marriage relationship.

Sign up today to receive your first set of four, never befo[re] published Christian romances. Send no money now; you w[ill] receive a bill with the first shipment. You may cancel at any tim[e] without obligation, and if you aren't completely satisfied wi[th] any selection, you may return the books for an immediate refun[d.]

Imagine. . .four new romances every four weeks—two histor[i-] cal, two contemporary—with men and women like you who lo[ng] to meet the one God has chosen as the love of their lives. . .all f[or] the low price of $9.97 postpaid.

To join, simply complete the coupon below and mail to th[e] address provided. **Heartsong Presents** romances are rated G f[or] another reason: They'll arrive *Godspeed!*